PRAISE FOR
RACE AGAINST TIME

"It is said sport is a microcosm of life. Bill Roushey did a wonderful job of demonstrating such with the tale he threads in this book. It is not often, the sport of cross country running becomes a storyline for a book. Roushey uses his excellent creative writing and storytelling skills to develop intersecting plotlines that will hold the attention of both the familiar and unfamiliar to the sport of cross country. Running is but part of the setting and not the real story of this book. Roushey blends the characters' personalities with their day-to-day struggles of balancing life's successes and failures, while navigating the mysteries of young love. It is a story of perseverance that conveys many of life's truths."

— ***Dr. Craig Hayward,*** EdD.
Retired University Professor and Coach

***

"*The Race Against Time* is a heart-warming story of college athleticism, deep love, and, above all, the way God works in the lives of all of His children to guide them to the path He intends for their lives. I thoroughly enjoyed Roushey's narration of the triumphs and pitfalls of competing at a college level, and the Christ-centered romance really takes the cake for me. I think all of Roushey's readers will learn more about the power of surrendering their desires to the Lord and how trusting in Him will always allow things to work out for the best, even if it's not how you expect—I know I certainly have."

— ***Branwyn M. Wilkinson,*** MSL,
Assistant Director of Alumni Engagement at RWU

"A delightful portrayal of where faith and determination intersect with the sparks of love, and where overcoming one's past often requires a willingness to trust in others who truly know you. The author takes you on a journey of hope, connection, and fun, while also reaching into the depths of the transformative power of God."

— *Kimberly Brittin,* Operations Director, Pearce Church

❧

"This story grabbed my attention right from the first chapter. Using the metaphor of cross country running to parallel our Christian walk was extremely effective to demonstrate our need for teammates, friends, and coaches to encourage us to reach our goals. Great character development with Carson's friends and soul mate. You made me want to know them. Kudos to Bill Roushey—great writing!"

— *Sandy Pickering*

❧

"From the beginning to the end of this book, I was captured by Carson's story. I appreciated how he shared his spiritual journey throughout the book and shared Bible verses that were important to him. His determination to succeed in life and love kept the story alive and interesting."

— *Ester Skiff*

THE RACE AGAINST TIME

THE RACE AGAINST TIME

A NOVEL

WILLIAM ROUSHEY, JR.

THE RACE AGAINST TIME

Author's Note

This is a work of fiction inspired by true events. Names and locations have been changed to give parties a measure of anonymity. The actual institution where the story unfolds remains unnamed, not out of fear of reprisal or to cause embarrassment, but to give readers a sense that this could be their university and therefore their story. Where actual institutions are mentioned, it is the author's attempt to add a measure of realism to the story. May all who read this story come to understand the power of forgiveness.

The views and opinions expressed in this book are those of the author and do not necessarily reflect the official policy or position of Illumify Media Global.

Scripture quotations marked TLB are taken from The Living Bible. Copyright © 1971. Used by permission of Tyndale House Publishers, a Division of Tyndale House Ministries, Carol Stream, Illinois 60188. All rights reserved.

Published by
Illumify Media Global
www.IllumifyMedia.com
"Let's bring your book to life!"

Paperback ISBN: 978-1-964251-75-2

Typeset by Art Innovations (http://artinnovations.in/)
Cover design by Debbie Lewis

Printed in the United States of America

Dedication

To Divine Providence, because when God answers prayers, it's sometimes not just a simple answer but layers upon layers of answers, like ripples spreading out on the surface of the water. God intervenes in the lives of his children to accomplish his perfect will.

So take a new grip with your tired hands,
stand firm on your shaky legs, and mark out a straight,
smooth path for your feet so that those who follow you,
though weak and lame, will not fall and hurt themselves
but become strong.

—Hebrews 12:12–13

CHAPTER ONE

*T*he year was 1979. A time when pay phones, vinyl record albums, muscle cars, and citizen band (CB) radios were commonplace. Handwritten letters were delivered by mail. It was a simpler time when college students conducted research using a card catalog found in the library and term papers were either typed or written out by hand. Students had yet to be exposed to personal computers, smartphones, and the internet. For a young man named Carson it was a time of personal discovery. He considered himself a byproduct of the Jesus Movement and a Bible called *The Way*.

Carson was a university student poised to embrace his senior year with unbridled enthusiasm. He was an inch shy of six feet tall and carried 145 pounds on his lean frame. On most days during the summer, he dressed in cutoff jeans, a T-shirt, and his favorite running shoes. Wavy locks of brown hair covered his head, and his hazel eyes peered out at the world through the rose-tinted lenses of his wire-rimmed glasses.

He had no goals save one: to acquire the diploma he'd mortgaged his future for. He loved the sense of community he'd found at the university. It was his adopted home. He cherished his closest friends like siblings. Despite the joy he felt whenever the university came to mind, Carson was hounded by a solitary thought from his past.

One day you will leave this place and everything you hold dear, and then you will find yourself alone.

Like many university students, Carson suffered through a season of doubt. During his sophomore year, questions surfaced in his mind he couldn't let go of. Why was he here? Would the education he gained from his college experience be worth the financial cost?

Eventually, Carson lost his way. He became indifferent to his studies and focused on the social aspects of college life instead. He soon found himself on academic probation. Doubt completely overwhelmed him by the end of his sophomore year, and he made a hasty decision to drop out.

He had never felt so alone during the three months he spent working as a tire changer instead of attending the university. Contemplating his future while he worked for minimum wage proved to be a wake-up call. During his time away, Carson took to running along the streets near his parents' suburban home because it brought him a measure of peace. He talked to God while he ran because it nourished his soul.

As his mind began to clear, it occurred to him that he had never fully applied himself to his studies. While the social experiment called "college" had served to liberate him from his parents' governance, his mistake was prioritizing fun over learning.

The more time he spent away from the university, the clearer the picture became until he resolved that he would return and finish what he started. Now, one and a half years since his return, though it was difficult, he'd managed to find a balance between studying and having fun. His grade point average inched upward. Missing a semester and changing his major from social work to biology meant that he'd had to spend an extra year at the university, but it didn't seem to matter now that the finish line was in sight.

Carson was finally a senior, but in the back of his mind he knew he was in a race against time. Failed relationships from the past eighteen months had cost him the chance to find the happiness he longed for that might lead to marriage. He had only himself to blame. His selfish and sometimes reckless behavior brought pain into not only his life but the lives of those who cared about him. He had been a desperado of sorts, clinging to the hit song of the same name by the Eagles as his anthem. The line "You better let somebody love you before it's too late" haunted him. That is, until the end of his junior year when he vowed to let God have control of his life. But as a young man with a tainted past attending a small Christian university, he had a tough road of redemption ahead of him. Carson vowed his senior year would be different.

He missed being away from his college friends during the summer months and anxiously awaited the start of his senior year. He wondered how Sunny was getting along with his on-campus summer job. When he visited Sunny earlier this summer, Sunny had been overwhelmed with landscaping assignments. Carson hoped this time it would be different. The two of them worked different shifts, Carson for the plastics factory and Sunny for the university, which had limited their interaction during the month of July.

Carson felt like stretching his legs after being confined to a molding machine for the past eight hours. So, on the final day of July, he left the noise of the plastics factory and walked over to the slumbering university. It was a fifteen-minute walk under a cloudless sky from the factory to Sharpes Hall, the dorm where Sunny was living, but long enough for the bright summer sun to scorch his skin.

Carson knocked on the opened door to Sunny's room. He spotted his friend standing in front of his stereo system, fiddling with it. Sunny was known for sporting a slow drawn-out smile even when the occasion didn't call for one. He was two inches taller than Carson and had a gangly appearance that made him easy to spot in a crowd. In addition to his smile, he had hard-to-tame locks of curly brown hair and large feet.

Sunny had a way of injecting humor into any situation. As if on cue, Sunny greeted Carson with an exaggerated, startled look. He slapped his hand over his heart and stumbled backward several steps.

"How's the job going, Sunny?" Carson asked, trying not to laugh at Sunny's antics.

"You wouldn't believe how dead this place is during the summer," Sunny replied.

"I can imagine. So what's new, anything?"

"I've decided to go out for cross-country this fall."

"What are you talking about. You're slower than a turtle," Carson replied, observing that Sunny carried a bit more weight than one would expect to find on a cross-country runner.

"Hey, I kept up with you when we were running from campus security."

"That was a game we played for fun."

"Well, I'm going for it," Sunny said. "You should join me."

"I don't know, Sunny. I practiced with the team last year until I was declared ineligible. Are you sure you're up for it? As I remember it, the practices were brutal."

"I'm ready for anything! You know why?"

"This ought to be good," Carson said, smiling. "Go ahead, enlighten me."

"It's my senior year and my last chance to do something memorable."

"There's got to be more to it than that, Sunny. You could join the drama club if you wanted to be remembered."

"Since you asked, there happens to be another reason," Sunny responded, flashing his trademark smile.

"What are you up to? Come on, out with it."

"Girls notice guys who are on sports teams."

Carson started laughing. "You seriously expect me to believe that?"

"Don't laugh, I'm serious."

"I tell you what, Sunny, if that's how easy it is to find a girlfriend, I'll go out for the team."

"Now you're making fun of me."

"I'm sorry, Sunny, but you walked right into that one."

Carson's heart went out to Sunny because he hadn't had the same luck attracting girls that Carson had. But Carson had wasted most of those opportunities, which put them both in the same boat—alone.

Sunny jammed his hands in his pockets. "Do you want to hang around for a while and listen to some music? This place could stand a little livening up."

"Nah, I'd better get going. I promised my mother I'd be home in time for supper."

Carson walked back to the factory to collect his car. He thought about his conversation with Sunny as he drove home in his 1972 Dodge Demon he'd recently had restored. All humor aside, something about the idea appealed to him. The truth was, he hadn't given up on running. He enjoyed his brief stint with cross-country last year before being kicked off the team over some silly regulation having to do with the number of course credits he'd taken over the previous twelve months. Missing one semester of college had come back to bite him. Casual running was not the same as cross-country racing, however. He found himself taking inventory of the various road races he'd participated in over the past twelve months. Five races did not seem like a lot, and most of them were less than five miles in length.

Whether he wanted to admit it or not, competing ran in his blood. Every year he'd competed in almost every intramural sport on campus. The one thing Carson lacked from his college experience, however, was a varsity letter, and to Sunny's point, time was running out. He resolved to go visit the cross-country coach tomorrow to see what his chances were.

He found the cross-country coach sitting in his office behind an aging oak desk and leafing through a stack of papers. His office was small, and he had barely enough room to walk around his desk. In addition to the desk, two vinyl-covered chairs with chrome legs straight out of the 1960s accommodated any visitors. Several plaques adorned the walls of his office. Apparently, Coach was a serious runner back in the day.

Last year was Coach's rookie year. He came to the university fresh out of graduate school. Now, with a year of coaching and recruiting under his belt, Coach projected a look of confidence when Carson made eye contact. The new and improved version of the coach possessed the same youthful face, slight build, and sandy brown hair. He rose from his chair when Carson walked into his office.

"Carson, it's good to see you again," Coach said, extending his hand. "What can I do for you?"

"Can I talk to you for a minute?" Carson asked.

"Certainly."

"I was thinking about trying out for the team this year."

"Do you have enough credit hours to compete? If I remember right, last year you were declared ineligible."

"I didn't realize that missing a semester would mess up my chances. My course load is right where it needs to be, and I'm on schedule to graduate in June."

"It's a little late to be making this decision, don't you think? Practice starts in four weeks."

"I love to run, Coach," Carson replied, pausing to choose the right words before continuing. He decided he might as well be honest with him. "I'd like to be able to contribute to the team and earn a varsity letter."

"Your reasons are admirable, but you should know that we already have a strong team on paper this year. It's nothing like the team I inherited last year."

Carson swallowed the lump forming in his throat. "I . . . I think that's great."

"I don't want to discourage you from trying out, but if you don't think you can do the workouts, there's no point in joining us. At last count there are thirteen runners trying out, including several talented freshmen. Not everyone will receive a letter at the end of the season."

"I understand."

"How many miles have you run this summer, Carson?"

"Not as many as I'd like. I've been working full-time at the factory across the street."

"To be a successful cross-country runner you need to log a lot of miles over the summer months—hundreds of miles. Those miles determine how successful you will be in the fall."

"I didn't know that," Carson said sheepishly.

When Carson left the coach's office, he noticed his shirt was wet with sweat under the armpits. He hadn't realized how nervous he was talking to Coach. It occurred to him that this team didn't need him. After listening to Coach talk, he realized he was woefully unprepared for what he might face if he decided to run with the team. Carson had a decision to make. He could fight an uphill battle with a slim chance of succeeding or forget about it altogether and focus on his studies. Just when he was ready to move on, another thought occurred to him. Sunny was one of the guys trying out for the team. If Sunny could make the team, then he could too. Carson felt a twinge of enthusiasm pinch his soul.

Carson acknowledged that he'd waited too long to go to see Coach. But he couldn't let go of the idea of going out for cross-country. Why else had he kept running after he was declared ineligible? Carson pondered a passage from the Bible he'd read recently; it was from the ninth chapter of Ecclesiastes. It seemed to fit the quandary he found himself in.

"Whatever you do, do well. . . . The swiftest person does not always win the race . . . . It is all by chance, by happening to be at the right place at the right time" (Ecclesiastes 9:10–11).

An unexpected purpose for clinging to the remaining days of summer sprang to mind. Today, August first, he would start training to run cross-country. Carson was determined to make use of every remaining day of summer vacation.

The weather in August in Upstate New York was hot and muggy. It was the time of year when the leaves on the trees lost their glossy appearance; they curled and clung to drooping branches. Sod, once lush and green, became stained with patches of dead or dying grass, giving it the appearance of a dirty carpet. Carson's soul, like the natural world around him, thirsted for the arrival of the September.

Training became an immediate priority for him. Occasional runs turned into daily workouts, rain or shine. Three-mile jogs became forty-minute training sessions. He pushed himself harder than he ever had before. As if to steel himself and affirm his commitment, he went to a barber and got a brush cut. His short hair was not likely to get him noticed by the girls, but he wasn't Sunny. He was running for a college letter, not a girlfriend. In his mind, this act was a necessity given his attempt to train in the stifling hot summer weather. He reminded himself it would all be for naught if he couldn't finish the workouts. The prospect of failure fueled his desire to succeed.

CHAPTER TWO

arson sighed when he set foot on campus one day late in the afternoon a little more than a week before the start of the academic year. This was his fifth homecoming in as many years. The feeling never got old for him.

Only athletes and resident advisors (RAs) were permitted to arrive early, leaving the campus nearly deserted. Carson shook off the eerie feeling he got entering the nearly empty dorm. The humid air abated somewhat when he entered the shadowy confines of his sterile dorm room. A set of bunk beds, two dressers, two desks, and two lighted mirrors were all standard issue. One of the walls in his room served as a closet.

Carson parted the heavy draperies to let natural light flood the room. He peered out over the campus from the second floor and absorbed the calm blanketing the landscape. A courtyard spread out before him, separating his building from an identical one next to it. The two buildings, North and South Halls, were referred to by the students as "the quads" because each two-story structure had dorm rooms on each end. A large lounge and an apartment for a resident director (RD) occupied the center portion of each building. RDs served as advisors to the students and were responsible for monitoring their behavior as well as their safety. RAs were students who reported to the RD. They were often called spies by their peers because they were the eyes and ears of the RD. There were four RAs in North Hall.

This was Carson's second year in North Hall. It was the only dormitory on campus that housed men and women in the same building, albeit on opposite ends. It was not unheard of for men to raid the women's dorm or vice versa. Though the root causes for such raids were rarely established, they usually involved a student and his or her friends vying for the attention of a member of the opposite sex.

A mechanical humming noise caught Carson's attention. It came from a mini refrigerator shoved into the closet beneath his roommate's clothes. He searched through his belongings for the lunch his mother had packed for him and put it in the fridge.

Carson longed to be reunited with his roommate, a Florida boy named Boris, who uttered the strangest expressions. They had roomed together for the past two years. Carson noticed he had already staked his claim to the lower bunk. Carson called him by his nickname, Mr. Trees, a holdover from their CB radio days. The nickname stuck to him like a statically charged piece of Styrofoam. Mr. Trees was one of the RAs in North Hall.

Mr. Trees was a barrel-chested man about five and a half feet tall. He loved watching baseball on the television but wasn't fleet-footed enough to play. Mr. Trees was studying to be a minister of the gospel, while Carson was pursuing a degree in the sciences.

Mr. Trees was a cherished friend, and Carson owed him a debt of gratitude because he had reached out to Carson at a time when he was wrestling with his future. Ultimately, it was Mr. Trees who convinced him to return to campus and resume his education.

Carson noticed a sneaker sitting on his desk. A note peaked out from under it.

"Shy Guy, I've gone to help Clara get settled in her room. I'll catch up with you after dinner. Keep the night open. Chow."

It had been a while since anyone referred to him by his CB radio handle. The memory of communicating with Mr. Trees using CB radios gave him a warm feeling, but it also reminded him of the time he was separated from the university. Mr. Trees used to chat with him over the radio late at night from the campus while he sat in his Dodge Demon parked in the driveway of his parents' house. Thankfully, Carson belonged on campus now and was about to start the grand finale of his college experience.

It figures that Mr. Trees would be with Clara. The two of them were practically engaged. Wasn't it just like him to find a way into the girls' dorm without getting himself into trouble. Carson chuckled at the thought of RAs bending the rules. He suspected the sneaker pinning the note to his desk offered a clue as to what Mr. Trees had planned for the evening.

Since he'd started a daily running routine, Carson's body seemed to notify him when it was time for a workout. He wasn't about to break his streak of running every day during the month of August. Instead of changing into his usual garb of cutoffs and a ratty T-shirt, he donned a brand-new pair of running shorts and tank top. If he was going out for the team, he needed to look the part.

Carson chose a mile-and-a-half route for his workout, involving the three roads that formed a triangle around the university. Main Street offered a gradual rising grade; Vine Street presented him the challenge of a short, steep hill before leveling out; and Townline Drive featured a downhill slope all the way back to Main. Carson remembered from last year when he trained with the team that these roads were also part of the cross-country course. He intended to complete this circuit three times.

He relaxed his stride and focused on controlling his breathing. He drew in a long breath and expelled it slowly. Minutes into his run, Carson began to perspire. The humidity in the air prevented the sweat from evaporating from his body and made his skin feel clammy. He forced his mind to blot out the troublesome humidity as he ran.

Carson thought about how happy Mr. Trees and Clara were. He wondered if he'd ever get to experience that same kind of happiness. He'd been close a couple of times, but one thing or another derailed each opportunity. Compatibility was just too hard to figure out on a handful of dates. Understandably, each person tried to put their best foot forward. Only time could expose a person's character flaws and dim the blinding light of infatuation.

He rounded the sharp corner at the intersection of Townline and Main. His long-distance breathing pattern became a natural rhythm and fed oxygen to the muscles in his legs. He gently swung his arms as his legs found their stride. A song he'd written during his time away from the university came to mind. Carson used it for motivation when he ran alone.

It was a misty spring morning, the air chilled me to the bone.
I wonder why I'd ever come here all alone.
In the openness of the woodland screamed the quiet air.
I stopped to remember the mad world out there.

I grabbed for my jacket as I headed out the door.
The battle I was waging was really a mental war.
My mind seemed so cloudy, as troubles ruled my life.
As time slipped through my fingers, I sought an answer to my strife.

This world isn't so awful,
There's still some good to be found.
It's the trouble that lies ahead,
All the problems in my head,
That can crumble a man into nothing.

I spotted a weathered stump ahead, just off the worn dirt trail.
The pressure had gotten to me, my outlook seemed rather pale.
By now the sun was glowing red and warming up the air.
The solution I discovered was the hope that lies in prayer.

This world isn't so awful,
There's still some good to be found.
No more troubles lie ahead,
No more problems in my head,
I've put them in the arms of God.

Carson was a different person than he was just a few short months ago. He was learning to give his worries about the future to God. The only way he could do that was to draw nearer to him.

God, thank you for guiding me back to the university. I confess I don't fully understand your purpose for bringing me back here. Something in my heart tells me I'm here for something more than a diploma. God, thank you for my friends Mr. Trees and Clara; please bless their future together.

And, God, you know the loneliness that haunts me. Please help me with that. Guide my footsteps this year. Give me strength as I run with the cross-country team. This is my last year to get things right. Please help me not to ruin this opportunity.

A verse came to mind, one of his favorites, as if planted there by God: "'For I know the plans I have for you,' says the Lord. 'They are plans for good and not for evil, to give you a future and a hope'" (Jeremiah 29:11).

Carson felt a heaviness in his legs build as he pushed his way up the hill on Vine Street. He was told that this area was once an apple orchard half a century ago. It was nothing but neatly spaced houses now. He shortened his stride and pumped his arms. His breathing became labored, so he drew in long, slow breaths. After cresting the hill, he lengthened his stride once again. The stiffness in his legs eased as the downward slope of Townline propelled him back to the intersection of Main.

He was completely drenched after three laps and headed back to the dorm for a shower. His muscles relaxed under the refreshing stream of water. Carson got dressed and decided to scout out the dorm.

One of the benefits of arriving on campus early was being able to commandeer any furniture in the common areas of the dorm left over from the previous year. The hallway on his floor of the dorm was oval shaped. A pair of bathrooms occupied the inside of the oval, whereas dorm rooms lined the outside. The hallway was deserted save an accent table, a Barcalounger, a couple of desk chairs, and a sofa. *A sofa!* It was the same full-size sofa he and Mr. Trees had rescued from Vine Street last year. It had a floral pattern his grandmother would be proud of. But more importantly, it didn't smell.

He dragged the sofa back to his room, stood it on end, and forced it though the doorway. Unfortunately, the sofa took up most of the remaining space in the room. Additionally, it required anyone entering their room to veer sharply around it to get to the desks and bunk bed.

Mr. Trees will be happy to see this again, Carson thought.

Carson grabbed his lunch out of the refrigerator and gobbled it down. The few calories he consumed would have to do for now. He'd have to go shopping with Mr. Trees later. He stretched out on the couch and pondered who he was likely to meet this semester before he drifted off to sleep. The afternoon gave way to evening, and the sky darkened.

Carson woke with a start. The sofa he was sleeping on pitched forward almost spilling him out on to the floor. He had a visitor.

"What in the world is this?" Mr. Trees exclaimed as he struggled back to his feet after colliding with the sofa, which blocked his entry into the room. He flicked on the overhead light and was startled at the sight of Carson rising from the sofa.

"What does it look like?" Carson replied. "Don't you remember it?"

"It'll make a nice burglar alarm, that's for sure," Mr. Trees said, flashing a grin. "Great to see you again, Carson. Clara was fond of this piece of furniture. She'll be happy to know you were able to save it."

"When are you two going to get engaged anyway?"

"I haven't figured out when it will happen yet, but you'll be one of the first to know."

"Why is there a sneaker sitting on my desk?"

"I couldn't come right out and ask you to go out on a midnight prowl with me, could I?"

"I don't know what they were thinking when they made you an RA. Isn't an RA supposed to walk the straight and narrow path so they can turn other people in? You can't be doing that stuff now."

"Are you implying that I'm a spy?"

"Hey, you said it, I didn't."

"I can do anything I want, you know, just as long as I don't get caught."

"This might be a good time to bring up the last conversation I had with your girlfriend. She made me promise her that I'd keep you out of trouble this year. She wants you to graduate."

"But my bachelor days are numbered, Carson. Didn't you promise me we'd have fun this year?" Mr. Trees replied. "I believe your exact words were, 'Let's go out with a bang!'"

"Why do you insist on doing that to me?"

"Doing what?"

"Putting me in the middle between you and Clara," Carson answered. "Okay, I'll go out with you tonight, but I can't stay out too late because I have my first cross-country practice tomorrow morning."

"Well, this will be a good warm-up for you then!"

The warmth of their laughter filled the room with an air of happiness. Carson and Mr. Trees were together again. They once joked about writing a memoir one day chronicling their adventures over the past several years; the dynamic duo planned to call themselves Husky and Starch.

Slightly after midnight that evening, the hour most students would normally be taking shelter in their dorm rooms, Carson and Mr. Trees slipped out into the night. Aside from breaking curfew, there was never any criminal intent in their outings. Their aim amounted to nothing more than alluding campus security while they moved about the campus under the cover of darkness. Occasionally, they'd pay a visit to a coed, but those visits had been all but eliminated now that Mr. Trees and Clara were an item.

Their first order of business was locating campus security, which was comprised of a single night watchman named Walter. He circulated around the campus inserting a key into a clock of some kind that he carried on his belt. He did this every time he entered a building. If they knew where the watchman was, then they could move about more freely.

Walter had a friendly face with graying slicked-back hair. Working the nightshift and sleeping during the day gave his sun-starved skin a ghostly white tone. He was a quiet man who hardly said a word to anyone. Carson was brave enough once to eat lunch at his table in the dining hall. He found him to be a genuinely nice man.

They spotted Walter driving through the center of campus. Carson and Mr. Trees dove behind a low retaining wall in the courtyard outside their dorm when his car passed by.

"That was close! I think we're getting a little rusty," Carson said.

"Yeah," Mr. Trees replied. "Hey, Carson, I promised Clara we would stop by tonight."

"That's clear across campus. We'd better wait until Walter gets out of his car and away from that spotlight he has in his vehicle."

"Clara says she wants to come out with us tonight."

"What? Are you crazy? You're both RAs. If they catch you two out after curfew before the semester even starts—"

Mr. Trees cut off Carson before he could finish. "Calm down, Shy Guy. I promised her, okay?"

The two hooligans moved like military figures advancing behind enemy lines. They hid behind a tree, sprinted to a hedgerow, and dove behind a large boulder before finally making it to the corner of the dining hall. For the next twenty minutes they were like cartoon characters playing a cat-and-mouse game with the watchman, who had no idea he was playing, hiding behind any object that would give them cover. Walter eventually headed away from the direction they planned to go. Once they were in the clear, they crossed Townline Drive under a streetlight. Clara's dorm now was in sight.

Mr. Trees tapped lightly on the window of Clara's room. Carson stifled a laugh as Mr. Trees tried to assist Clara as she exited through an open window. The two of them landed in a heap on the ground.

Clara was equal to Mr. Trees in height. She had straight brown shoulder-length hair and pretty brown eyes. She had a dry sense of humor, but more importantly, she had a calming effect on Mr. Trees.

"Hi, Clara, nice to see you again," Carson said, helping her to her feet.

"Did my honey tell you I wanted to come out with you boys tonight?" she said, giving Carson a hug.

"Yes, he did, but not until after we were outside."

Clara laughed. "Don't be mad at him, Carson."

"I'm afraid there's not much happening tonight. There's hardly a soul on campus," Carson replied.

"That's the only reason I agreed to let her come out with us," Mr. Trees claimed.

"Well, let's go see what Walter is up to, and then I'm afraid I'll have to call it a night. I need to get my beauty rest," Carson said, smiling.

CHAPTER THREE

All prospective cross-country runners were to gather in the gym, which the students affectionately called "the pit," a basketball court constructed in the basement of Sharpes Hall, one of the oldest buildings on campus. A three-foot-wide balcony encircled the court, contributing to the oddity of the landmark. The pit caused more injuries than any other place on campus, including the soccer field, because there was less than three feet of clearance separating the court from the concrete block walls lining the court. Carson himself suffered a sprained ankle two years earlier while trying out for the junior varsity basketball team. Twenty plus years ago, when Carson's father attended the university, the pit was the venue for varsity basketball games. More recently, however, the university played its games at a local high school.

Carson arrived early for cross-country practice.

"I'm glad you decided to come, Carson," Coach said. "I'm sorry things didn't work out for you last year."

"I guess you could say I'm ready to finish what I started," Carson answered.

"Hey, Carson! Looks like you took me up on my offer," Sunny shouted down from the balcony.

"I couldn't let you get all the girls, Sunny," Carson shot back.

"Girls?" Coach asked.

"It's not worth the time it would take to explain," Carson replied, laughing.

Carson and Sunny found a spot on the large wrestling mat Coach had dragged out of storage. One by one, young men trickled into the pit and found a place on the mat. Coach had to be excited with the turnout when fourteen runners showed up.

Coach began by telling the student athletes a little bit about himself. He said he ran cross-country for Spring Arbor College one of the university's sister colleges. While he was there, the team competed for a national championship—twice. After getting a master's degree in education, he felt led by God to pursue coaching at a Christian college. His opportunity came when the university's current coach retired. He came here with the idea of passing on his knowledge to the runners he coached.

"Believe it or not, this university dominated the New York state championship meets back in the 1960s. No one could beat them. Gentlemen, I intend for our university to once again be included in the conversation of good cross-country schools. That starts today with this team," Coach declared.

Carson noticed a hush had fallen over the room. Coach was nothing like the coach he knew from last year. The new and improved version was organized, motivated, and determined to put together a winning team.

Coach continued, "Look around the room. These men are your teammates. Over the next several weeks you will get to know them. I want you to run with teammates you can keep pace with. If we're going to win any meets this year, you'll need to support each other. One runner might be able to win a race, but it takes a team to win a meet.

"During a race, I may be asking you to mark an opposing runner and find a way to beat him. Never allow yourself to get caught running alone. That's when you're the most vulnerable, and it can be a recipe for disaster.

"For the next five days, starting today, we'll be training twice a day, rain or shine. There will be a long-distance workout in the morning followed by a technique-inspired workout after lunch. Friday afternoon, I've arranged an overnight stay for us in Bristol, New York, on the property the university owns. A week from tomorrow we'll race in a non-scoring meet at Geneseo. How we run there will give us an idea of where we stand as a team.

"Let's start our practice this morning with fifty sit-ups. Running develops the muscles in your legs and lower back. Sit-ups will strengthen your core and help stave off possible back problems later."

Fifty sit-ups were easily doable for Carson. He thought about doing more but decided against it. The less attention he drew to himself, the better. At least until after he got past the first week of practice.

Coach beamed with pride as fourteen runners followed him down Main Street. He turned off Main and headed south on a country road. The pace Coach dictated was quicker than what Carson was used to. He couldn't believe the ease with which Coach ran.

After three miles, the team fragmented into two distinct groups. The faster group included Coach and six of the best runners. They maintained a consistent pace and began pulling away from the second group, who were starting to suffer.

Carson tried to run at the front of the second group of eight runners. Two miles later his breathing became so labored he had no choice but to slow down. He dropped back through the ranks until he found himself hanging on to the tail of the second group. Carson noticed Sunny stumbling along beside him and offered him an encouraging smile. Though his lungs were screaming at him, he refused to quit running. One thought occupied Carson's mind for the rest of the run. *I can't be the last runner to finish.*

Carson pushed himself hard when the university came into view. He was determined to position himself ahead of some of the slower runners on the off chance that Coach might be using the eight-mile run to evaluate the team. Deep down Carson believed that what he had just endured would pale in comparison to what lay ahead. Sunny's trademark smile was nowhere to be found when he finished. They had both suffered greatly.

The afternoon practice began outdoors under one of the oldest maple trees on campus. The towering arbor provided a huge canopy of shade, some twenty-five feet in diameter. Fifty more sit-ups were required before the next workout.

"I want you to add wall and hurdle stretches to your warm-up routine. Too many runners are lost each season due to injuries," Coach said. "This afternoon we are going to practice our hill-running technique. You'll be running up and down a lot of hills this season, especially on the harder courses."

Coach continued, "To attack a hill, shorten your stride, lean into it, and pump your arms to help power your legs. When you're running downhill, let the slope carry you, lengthen your stride, but keep your body centered over your legs. Some runners like to attack, or press their pace, uphill; others attack downhill, running with reckless abandon. It's up to you to figure out which way works best for you."

Carson expected a van to show up at any moment to chauffer them to the appointed hill. Instead, Coach wheeled out a bicycle with a banana seat and said, "Follow me."

Two and a half miles later they stood at the base of a hill that rose for a quarter of a mile. Carson thought it would make a great toboggan run during the winter months. Coach repeated his instructions for proper hill-running technique.

"When I blow the whistle, head up the hill at a consistent pace, and when you reach the top, turn and stride back down. Keep an eye out for traffic. When you reach the bottom of the hill, cool down by jogging to Aldridge Road and back."

Coach blew a whistle, and runners headed single file up the hill. The afternoon sun beat down on them in a cloudless sky. It was a beautiful summer afternoon. Carson noticed bees buzzing around the flowering weeds growing along the shoulder of the road. Birds chirped at him from the hedgerows outlining the farmers' fields. There was no hint of a breeze.

Sweat pored off Carson as he powered up the hill. He tried in vain to quiet his breathing. By the time he reached the top of the hill, he was gasping for breath. The downhill run brought a bit of relief because the movement of his body created a slight breeze. Coach waited for the squad to reassemble after their cool down.

"Again!" Coach shouted.

The fastest runners approached the hill with almost the same measure of enthusiasm and speed. The rest of the runners labored up the hill at a much slower pace because they were still tired from the first climb.

Coach blew his whistle. "Again!"

Sunny and one other runner sat out the third attempt because they were still trying to catch their breath. Carson felt as if he was climbing the hill at a snail's pace. He let some of his teammates push past him. Even the best runners were feeling it by the time they reached the bottom of the hill. After Carson and his teammates completed their cool down, Coach passed out paper cups filled with water he drew from a jug strapped to his bicycle. Carson observed how quickly the best runners recovered. They had obviously run a lot of miles over the summer.

"This is the last hill today," Coach announced. "When you get to the top of the hill, keep going down to the end of the street and turn left. That road will lead you back to Main Street. I'll see you back at school."

Coach turned his bike around and headed back the way he came, thus avoiding the hill. Runners took their time pushing up the hill. Carson noticed some runners paused at the top of the hill to link up with the teammates they had run with that morning. He finished after a great deal of effort. When he crested the hill, he was surprised to see one of the freshman runners waiting for him.

"Hey Rookie! Why don't you run back with me?"

"What did you call me?" Carson asked, trying to catch his breath.

"Rookie. You're new to cross-country, aren't you?"

"Sort of," Carson replied.

"Word has it that you've never run a cross-country race."

"Who told you that?"

"I don't know his name, but I heard you call him Sunny earlier this morning."

"It figures," Carson said, but he was too exhausted to laugh. "Are you a Trekkie? I hope so because you remind me of one of the Star Trek characters. I think I'm going to call you Spock."

The freshman cackled, which brought a smile to Carson's face. The two shook hands.

"You're a dead ringer for him, you know. All you lack are the pointy ears," Carson added.

"Come on, Rookie, let's go home."

"Spock, you do realize I won't be able to keep up with you."

"True, but I'm not racing you today."

"Ha-ha."

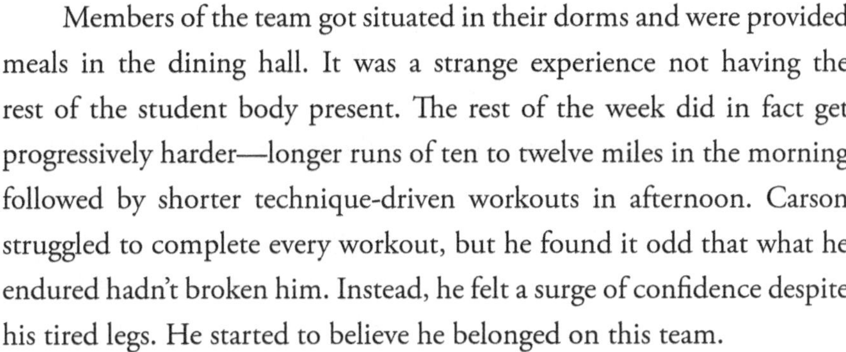

Members of the team got situated in their dorms and were provided meals in the dining hall. It was a strange experience not having the rest of the student body present. The rest of the week did in fact get progressively harder—longer runs of ten to twelve miles in the morning followed by shorter technique-driven workouts in afternoon. Carson struggled to complete every workout, but he found it odd that what he endured hadn't broken him. Instead, he felt a surge of confidence despite his tired legs. He started to believe he belonged on this team.

Carson and Sunny both made it through "hell week" without quitting. Carson's nickname, Rookie, stuck to him thanks to Sunny's incessant use of it. Carson found this ironic since he had more cross-country experience than Sunny did. Something about the way Sunny joked about him in front of the other runners irritated Carson. Was he just being Sunny, or did he detect a hint of jealousy? Rather than get upset, Carson decided to let it go.

If Carson had to guess, he would place himself about tenth fastest on the team. It was a far cry from being able to help the team win a meet or earn him a varsity letter. But it was too early to tell what could be gained by running near the back of the pack during the team's training workouts. He reminded himself that he believed God had a purpose for him being on the team.

He concluded that Sunny would undoubtedly be noticed by the girls on campus because he was a clown. What was Carson's goal now that he understood the situation he found himself in? He had no idea, but he wasn't about to quit.

There was a party atmosphere in the van as Coach drove the team to the Bristol property the university owned on top of a mountain. During the hour-long trip, nicknames were being assigned, and jokes were aplenty. Freshman, sophomore, junior, and senior runners were all interacting swimmingly. There wasn't a hint of class hierarchy. Coach absorbed all of what was being said without commenting.

The van got quiet when the gravel road they were driving on disappeared three-quarters of the way up the mountain. Eyes widened as the van followed a pair of tire ruts the rest of the way up. A huge timbered lodge suddenly appeared in a clearing. Adjacent to the lodge was a utility shed and a smaller traditionally built cottage.

The main lodge had four small bedrooms on the first floor and four more on the second. A wraparound balcony connected the upstairs bedrooms.

The center of the lodge was basically one enormous great room. A kitchen and bathroom occupied a small space in the rear, while a dining area occupied the middle section. A grand living room took up the rest of the space, which was furnished with sofas and side chairs that faced a massive stone fireplace. A huge chandelier hung from a vaulted ceiling. The lodge's most prominent feature, however, was the enormous head of a bull moose whose antlers dominated the open space above the fireplace.

Carson loved the setting, but unbeknownst to everyone else, this was not his first trip to the property. Four years earlier, he came as a freshman with a group of students for a social mixer, which allowed him to get better acquainted with some of his classmates. He made a second trip last year with his biology class to study the surrounding landscape.

Coach was surprised when he learned that Carson was no stranger to the place. He asked him to serve in a leadership role during their stay. This was the break Carson had been waiting for, a chance to do something meaningful for the team. He led his teammates over the wooded trails as the afternoon skies began to darken. Carson highlighted the fact that this type of habitat was ideal for black bears. He joked about bears being sighted nearby. Everyone seemed to lose interest in exploring the trails when darkness fell. It likely had something to do with his comment about the bears.

When they arrived back at the lodge, Carson helped Coach get the generator running. His teammates cheered when the lights came on. Later that evening Sunny started a pillow fight, which was brought to an abrupt end by Coach.

In the morning, Coach led the team in a devotional he'd prepared. He likened the races they would run to a spiritual journey each of them must take in life. He read a passage of Scripture from the book of Hebrews, one that Carson was familiar with.

"Since we have such a huge crowd of men of faith watching us from the grandstands, let us strip off anything that slows us down or holds us back, and especially those sins that wrap themselves so tightly around our feet and trip us up; and let us run with patience the particular race God has set before us. . . . If you want to keep from becoming fainthearted and weary, think about [Jesus'] patience as sinful men did such terrible things to him" (Hebrews 12:1–3).

Carson associated the crowd of men of faith watching from the grandstands with the crowd of spectators he was liable to see at their cross-country meets. He also thought about Christ's patience in the midst of his struggles, which gave him new insight into the struggle he would face when he raced. He affirmed his commitment to stay connected to God and fully rely on him, especially during the times when his strength would fail.

Coach reminded the team that they were part of a Christian university and were therefore ambassadors of the institution. He expected their conduct during the cross-country season to reflect that.

They had a light workout on the hiking trails after the devotional. Carson got a kick out of reminding everyone about the possibility of bears being in the area. As a result, everyone, with the exception Coach and Carson, appeared to run nervously through the woods. Carson smiled as he watched his teammates bunched in a tight group, constantly scanning the terrain and looking for any sign of movement.

During their stay, Carson met another freshman runner, whom Spock called Fly. Fly was four inches shorter than Carson and about twenty pounds lighter. He had a slight build, a bearded face, and an especially magnetic personality. From what Carson could tell, Fly was the fastest runner on the team. He literally ran like he had wings. Carson later learned that Fly was a high school state champion. Fly was given the nickname by another teammate named Einstein.

Carson already knew Einstein. He was a fourth-year senior and a science major. His grade point average, however, was far better than Carson's. He was about Carson's height and weight but was a much faster runner. Carson enjoyed calling him Einstein because he had tremendous respect for him.

Everyone on the team seemed to be getting along great, as evidenced by all the fun they were having. In just a short time, they had become a brotherhood of men. Joking ran rampant within the squad, but no one seemed to take offense to any of it. No matter what happened once the racing started, Carson knew that Fly, Spock, and Einstein would be his friends on and off the cross-country course.

When the cross-country team returned to the campus from their retreat, the incoming freshmen were moving about the campus. Carson's heart was warmed by the thought that the slumbering university was beginning to awaken. In a matter of hours, the upperclassmen would be arriving, and the overly enthusiastic freshmen would no longer have the place to themselves. Carson chuckled at the prospect of the RAs in the freshman dorms trying to maintain order during this type of party atmosphere. He gathered his gear and returned to his dorm room to relax before heading to the dining hall for dinner.

At dinner that evening the dining hall was exceptionally noisy. The room was buzzing with freshmen and upperclassmen who were making new friendships or renewing existing ones. It created an atmosphere charged with hope for what the new academic year might bring. Carson ate with the runners and enjoyed watching a half dozen freshman girls flirt with Fly. Judging from the girls' behavior in Fly's presence, Carson believed that if Fly wanted to run for class president, he'd easily win hands down.

CHAPTER FOUR

Carson pulled the windbreaker he was wearing over his head to ward off the light rain and hurried back to his room after supper. The semester would start in two days, and the dorm was anything but quiet. Students continued to return to campus one by one, and their exuberant voices echoed in the hallways as they reunited with friends. Carson joined the chorus, welcoming back a number of his friends. Contributing to the chaos was the music from several stereos, each playing a different type of music, giving the dorm a carnival atmosphere.

Back in his room, Carson occupied himself sorting through his clothes, placing some items on hangers and stowing the rest in drawers. He'd been too busy with cross-country practice and the retreat to properly arrange his belongings. He studied his reflection in the mirror above his dresser. Was he truly a different person this year? He hoped to show everyone who knew him that he was.

He set his stereo on top of his dresser and attached the wires to the speakers. Leafing through dozens of vinyl albums, he selected one of his favorites, *The Stranger* by Billy Joel. Many of the songs resonated with him, but "Vienna" had quickly become one of his favorites. Carson indeed had "so much to do and only so many hours in a day." As he sat at his desk arranging the supplies he'd brought from home, he heard a knock on the door.

"Come in," Carson shouted as he turned down the volume.

Fly appeared in the doorway.

"What can I do for you?" Carson asked.

"I stopped by to say hello. I'm your new neighbor," Fly replied.

"I thought you were staying in the Sharpes Hall. What happened?"

"Some sort of administrative error. They assigned three people to my room. When I got back from Bristol, the other two guys had already moved in. I found my stuff in a neat pile in the closet."

"Welcome to North Hall then. You're welcome in my room anytime."

"Where's your roommate?"

"Visiting his older brother in Pennsylvania," Carson answered. "You're welcome to stay."

"Nice sofa," Fly said, stretching himself out on it.

"Is it okay if I call you Fly because I don't know your real name?"

He laughed. "Yeah, that's fine. For the record my real name is Bart, short for Bartholomew. Don't they call you Rookie?"

"That was Sunny's idea. He can be a real pain sometimes, but he's a friend."

Carson found Fly interesting to talk to. It was refreshing to converse with a guy this talented who didn't possess an ounce of arrogance. Eventually the conversation turned to members of the opposite sex.

"I saw you talking to some cute girls at supper tonight," Carson said, smiling. "It looked like you were having a good time."

"I think they were just being friendly," Fly replied.

"It looked to me like they were flirting with you, from what I saw."

"They're cute, I'll give you that. But I'm not interested."

"Why not, if you don't mind my asking?" Carson countered.

"I have a girlfriend back home. Her name is Megan," Fly replied. "What about you, Carson, do you have a girlfriend?"

"Well, that's a touchy subject. I have girl 'friends,' but I can't see myself spending the rest of my life with any of them. Hopefully, someday I'll find Miss Right."

Fly joined Carson for a light run Sunday morning after breakfast. The sun was bright, moving in and out of the puffy white clouds that dominated the sky. Carson drew in cool morning air that carried a refreshing hint of fall. Leaves were starting to show signs of color, giving the landscape the look of an unfinished painting. To Carson's delight, students were milling about everywhere. It was great to see the campus alive again.

Carson took Fly to his church after they changed into street clothes. He and Fly were fast becoming friends. That afternoon Carson gave his new friend a nitty-gritty guided tour of the campus, highlighting the good and bad elements of the place, things the administration didn't highlight on the tours they gave.

Monday, Carson received word that Coach wanted to speak with him in his office before practice. A wave of nervousness flashed through his body, though he couldn't substantiate a reason for it. His new class schedule kept him busy all morning. After lunch he decided he'd better go find out what Coach wanted.

"Coach, you wanted to see me?"

"Come in, Carson. Have a seat."

"Sorry I didn't come earlier; it's been a busy morning."

"You are probably wondering why I called you in to see me."

"I hope I haven't done something wrong."

"Just the opposite, Carson. Whether you know it or not, you're doing a lot of things right."

Coach continued, "I wanted to thank you for your leadership at the retreat. This team needs leaders like you. Gifted runners like Bart can benefit from that kind of leadership on and off the course."

"We call him Fly," Carson replied, feeling a sense of relief. "It's hard to imagine me as a leader when I'm one of the last ones to finish the workouts. I wish I was performing better in practice."

"That's the other reason I wanted to talk to you," Coach responded. "You don't think you're improving, do you?"

"No."

"I can tell you that you are. You'll start seeing the results soon. Just keep pressing on toward the prize."

"That sounds biblical," Carson said with a bit of a nervous laugh.

"It is. Look up Philippians chapter three sometime."

"I will," Carson said, pulling a pen out of his pocket and writing "Phil 3" on his hand.

"Carson, before you go . . . you said you wish you were performing better. Let me give you something to think about. The workouts we are doing are intended to challenge the best runners on our team, and you are finishing them. What do you think that says about you?"

Carson paused. "So does this mean I'm on the team?"

"We are going to start the season with all fourteen runners since everyone completed the workouts. We're bound to lose some runners due to injury. Congratulations, Carson! Yes, you're part of the team!"

"Thanks, Coach," Carson replied, walking away with a bit of a spring in his step.

That afternoon, Coach excused anyone nursing an injury from practice. He kept the pace of the workout slow and used the opportunity to familiarize the team with their home course.

"You're going to hear opposing teams say this course is a bowl of spaghetti. We can use that to our advantage. All the different loops around the course are designed for the benefit of the spectators so they can see most of the race. It's to your advantage to get to know every inch of it."

❧

Tuesday afternoon Carson was a bundle of nerves riding in the van as it traveled through the rolling hills of New York State's Finger Lakes region. The harsh heat and stale colors of summer had given way to the lushness of autumn. Normally, the rural setting of vineyards and farms would have a calming effect on him, but anxiety clouded his mind and therefore his vision. Carson tried to muster courage from the uniform he wore: a white tank top and red shorts bearing the university's name and logo. Laughing and joking with his teammates seemed to help. That is, until they arrived on site and walked out onto the battlefield.

Carson tried to keep himself distracted, stretching and chatting with teammates. Coach disappeared into the sea of runners mingling on the athletic field. He returned several minutes later with a handful of numbered mylar sheets. Injuries had reduced the team to twelve men. Coach distributed the numbers along with enough safety pins to affix them to their jerseys. He reminded everyone not to overdo it. This was a non-scoring meet, and the team had a scoring meet in just a few days.

Carson had run several road races in the past but had never participated in a team event. He wondered if running for a team might add to the burden he already felt. Why did his first race have to be almost six and a half miles long? He found himself pacing, lost in thought, trying to convince himself that this race was no different than any he'd run before. Fly managed to sneak up on him.

"Hey, Rookie, are you okay?" Fly asked, startling him.

"I'm nervous, that's all," Carson responded, shaking his arms to relieve some of the stress.

"Don't let worry steal your energy."

"Good point. Are you ready, Fly?"

"Absolutely, this is what I came here for."

Fly was a different person when he put his game face on. Whether it was from confidence or concentration, Carson knew that his friend was ready for battle.

Ninety-four runners from nine different colleges and universities crowded the starting line. Carson wanted to remain anonymous, but the sun beating down on his shoulders made it feel like he was under a spotlight. He prayed that God would help him avoid the mayhem at the start of the race, runners crashing into each other as they scrambled for position.

When the starting pistol barked, the runners charged forward in unison. A wave of adrenaline swept over Carson, flushing the nervousness out of his system. The season, and his race with destiny, had begun.

During the opening moments of the race, the runners were so tightly packed together that Carson couldn't see the course ahead. He was being pushed along faster than he wanted to go. He looked down and noticed his feet were no longer on a grassy surface. They had transitioned to pavement. He breathed a sigh of relief when the runners slowly began to spread out, revealing the terrain ahead of him like a lifting fog.

A long continuous hill stretched out before him. He guessed it was three, possibly four, times the length of the hill they trained on. Carson recounted how he dreaded hill workouts.

This hill will be my undoing, he thought.

Carson battled with his mind and tried to focus on what Coach had taught them about running up a grade. The adrenaline still circulating through his body proved to be more of a hindrance than a help. It made his legs feel springy, forcing him to waste energy, bouncing on the balls of his feet and slowing down his progress. When the adrenaline finally subsided, his legs felt like someone had strapped weights to his ankles. A wave of panic flashed through his body. Was he going to finish this race?

He struggled to catch his breath, wanting to blame the runners ahead of him for sucking much-needed oxygen out of the air, but he knew this wasn't true. What could he do to gain control of his breathing? He searched for that quiet place deep within him where he talked to God.

God, calm me down so I can run this race. Please help me to figure out how to gain control of my breathing.

Carson used the same spirit that connected him to God to calm his hyperactive mind. He sucked in as much air as he possibly could and then pushed every ounce of it out of his lungs before drawing another deep breath. The outside world around him quieted, and the only sound he could hear was his own breathing.

His body screamed at him to break his stride and slow to a walk, but Carson's spirit pressed on. Moments later the grade leveled off. His eyes spotted a long chalk arrow on the asphalt that bent to the right. He willed his feet to follow it. The terrain transitioned to a loose cinder trail, which led him into a small patch of woods. The trail proved to be treacherous, and he stumbled over an exposed root. He continued to take slow, deep breaths. When the overhead canopy cleared, Carson found himself in a clearing. Another arrow directed him across a series of athletic fields. He spotted other runners off in the distance. The momentary distraction almost caused him to miss a partially trampled message on the grass.

Did that say two miles?

He continued to slow his pace. He was almost jogging now, which helped some of the heaviness in his legs to abate. His breathing slowly improved. Another arrow bent sharply to the right, directing him onto a campus road.

I must be headed back to the start he thought.

Carson picked up speed as the road fell away under his feet and snaked around the campus buildings. He found himself racing downhill, going faster than he wanted to. Another message appeared on to the road: "Three Miles."

He let his legs carry him faster and faster until he was on the verge of losing his balance. Time slowed dramatically as adrenaline once again flooded his body. Following a sharp bend in the road, Carson saw the finish line ahead. This confused him because he'd run only a little over three miles. His heart sank when he realized he had to run the route a second time.

The second uphill climb was harder than his first encounter with it. Even at a much slower pace, he used up most of the energy he needed to finish the race. Carson stumbled across the cinder trail, twice avoiding a fall. When he reached the grass, he could feel the drag on his feet. There was no spring left in his legs. He wanted the race to be over and released a frantic plea.

God, I need your strength! Don't let me fail. Don't let me fall.

The last downhill plunge was a blur. He focused solely on keeping himself upright. When he finally crossed the finish line, it felt like he had woken up from a bad dream. Carson was given the time of 46:34, nearly twelve minutes behind the first-place finisher.

As Carson struggled to catch his breath, twelve more runners crossed the finish line; four of them were teammates. The pain wracking his body seemed more tolerable when he learned he was the eighth fastest runner on the team. Perhaps he did deserve to be part of this team.

Out of the corner of his eye, he spotted Coach attending to a bloody scrape on Truman's shin. Carson knew little about his teammate because he'd mostly kept to himself at the retreat. Carson did learn that he was a transfer student, and Einstein said he had a sly sense of humor.

Carson reflected on the race as he walked around the athletic field attempting to revive his stiff legs. He looked heavenward and gave credit where it was due.

God, I am truly grateful. Thank you for enabling me to finish the race, for giving me hope when I had none, for giving me strength when I had nothing left.

Carson marveled that his pulse had stopped racing, his breathing had normalized, and some of his energy had returned by the time the team piled into the van. He concluded that perhaps Coach was right, that his training was having a positive effect on his results. Only his tired legs bore the aftereffects of the race.

That evening Carson ate supper in the dining hall with Mr. Trees, Clara, and several of Clara's fellow nursing students across two tables. The dinner conversation, if you could call it that, was a discussion regarding which student would make the best candidate for homecoming queen. This wasn't a pointless exercise, however, because the voting block of nursing students outnumbered every other academic major on campus, by far. Mr. Trees and Carson purposely tried to ignore them. That is, until Clara directed a question toward Carson.

"Carson, are you willing to be the escort for the senior nominee for homecoming queen?"

Mr. Trees started laughing so hard he couldn't stop.

"Why do I get the feeling that this is a setup?" Carson asked.

"It's a simple yes or no question," one of Clara's friends added.

"I guess that would depend on who it is," Carson answered.

"So, it's a yes then," another student abruptly concluded.

Carson decided he'd better start paying attention to the discussion since his name was now part of the conversation. Because the total student body numbered about six hundred students, he recognized most of the names being tossed about. He concluded that he was probably safe because the discussion seemed to be going nowhere. When Carson had finally heard enough, he gathered his dirty dishes, put them on a tray and headed to the dishwashing area.

When he arrived back in his room, Carson stretched out on his sofa and opened his Bible to Philippians 3. The words leaped off the page as he read them.

A Christian needed to keep "working toward" perfection or completeness, as demonstrated by Jesus Christ (Philippians 3:12). They did so by gripping tightly to their faith, forgetting what was in their past, and striving toward the future. The goal was to "reach the end of the race and receive the prize" (Philippians 3:14). Anyone who strives to do this must hold on to the progress they've already made.

The part about forgetting what was in the past certainly spoke to him. It was easy to apply this scripture to his running, particularly the part about holding on to the progress he'd already made. He understood the meaning of pressing on, gripping tightly to his training and faith for support. The words fed his soul, and he vowed to call on them in his hour of need.

It had been an exhausting couple of days for Carson at the beginning of the semester. He quickly settled into a routine. Each morning, he attended classes in the science building, ran with the cross-country team in the afternoon, and studied in the library for a few hours every evening. His routine ate up a substantial portion of his time. Any free time he did have was spent with Mr. Trees or Fly.

Friday evening there was a concert being held at the church adjacent to the campus. It featured the Wall Brothers Band. Carson asked Madison to go with him. She was a tall girl almost matching his height. When the guys in Sharpes Hall shamelessly published a list of the ten best-looking girls on campus, Madison was on the list, largely because she had very pretty eyes and a very cute face. He'd been trying for a couple of years to get her to go on a date with him, and she finally said yes.

Carson thought it was amusing how many of the senior nursing majors were suddenly interested in dating guys and working toward their Mrs. degree now that a bachelor of science degree in nursing was within sight. Some of the guys at the university referred to this phenomenon as bride fever.

Madison and Carson enjoyed the concert together and talked for a while afterward. He had a pleasant time with her, but she was too quiet for his liking. Carson was undecided as to whether he should ask her out again. He had a race to worry about, so he let the matter go.

CHAPTER FIVE

The weather Saturday morning was perfect for a race. A cloudy sky kept the temperature in the sixties. Fifty runners from six area colleges and universities gathered to compete in the Buffalo State Invitational. It was Carson's first scoring race. Carson heard that the course was flat and almost two miles shorter than the Geneseo course. This was music to his ears.

Once the race got underway, Carson drifted to the back of the pack of runners. He was determined not to tax his breathing early on. The absence of hills enabled him to control the rate at which he used his energy. Halfway into the race, he was encouraged by the fact that his legs remained fresh.

Unlike the Geneseo race, Carson chose to keep his eyes focused on the course ahead of him, which permitted him to see the position of the other runners. He drew encouragement from watching his teammates perform on the battlefield. Einstein, Spock, and Phantom (one of the team's better runners who had a knack of flying under the radar) maintained contact with their competitors. He also thought he caught a glimpse of Truman and Fly running with the leaders.

A shift occurred in Carson's thinking as the race played out before him. Where he once was concerned solely with self-preservation, he felt a willingness to sacrifice himself for the team's success should the opportunity present itself. He looked for one of his teammates to run with. He spotted Shorty a few seconds ahead of him. Shorty may have been five or six inches shorter than Carson, but he was his comparative equal, running with both heart and determination. Carson thought of Shorty as a true ladies' man—muscular, blond hair, and a face like Robert Redford's.

The two of them ran together for most of the remainer of the race. Their conversation was limited to just a few words of encouragement. As the race neared its completion, Shorty could no longer keep pace, and exhorted Carson to keep going and finish strong.

For Carson, running with Shorty was his first positive racing experience. As if to pay tribute to him, Carson pushed himself to the brink of exhaustion the final quarter mile and netted forty-fourth place. He was pleased with his time of 29:13, which was less than six minutes behind winning time. It finally occurred to him that all Coach expected was for his runners to put forth their best effort every race. For the first time, Carson saw that running on this team could make him a better person.

Since it was a scoring meet, the team's third-place finish proved to area colleges and universities that their team had risen from the ashes. Carson's status on the team had risen as well. He had become the seventh fastest runner on the team, and to his way of thinking he was now someone who could contribute.

～

One Sunday afternoon a month, a few of the boys' or girls' dorms were open to members of the opposite sex for three hours. North Hall was on the list for this month. Mr. Trees, one of the dorm's RAs, made arrangements with the first-floor RA to cover for him so he could spend some time with Clara, leaving Carson to host any visitors. Fly was the first person to appear.

"We should do something tonight to celebrate our good showing yesterday," Carson said.

"What did you have in mind?" Fly asked.

"Let's go out for some ice cream. We can go to Ho Jo's."

"Ho Jo's?"

"It's a worn-out joint that's open twenty-four hours about five miles from here. Students go there all the time just to hang out or study late at night."

As they were pondering who they should invite, four freshman girls dropped in to see Fly. Carson recognized a couple of them. They were part of the group that flirted with Fly in the dining hall.

"Is this your room?" one of them asked Fly.

"No, this is Carson's room, mine's next door," Fly replied.

"Fly and I were just trying to figure out who we could invite to go out with us for some ice cream tonight. We want to celebrate our great showing at Buffalo State yesterday. Fly here almost won the whole thing," Carson said.

Carson had to explain to the girls why the team called Bart *Fly*. Carson offered the girls his spot on the couch and moved to one of the desk chairs. Two of the girls jumped at the chance to sit on either side of Fly. They proceeded to tease and tickle him. The other two girls sat on Mr. Trees's bunk. They listened as Carson and Fly talked about the team and the fun they had on their trips to Bristol, Geneseo, and Buffalo.

After about an hour, one of the girls sitting on the bunk said, "We should probably get going."

"What time are you going out for ice cream?" one of the girls sitting next to Fly asked.

"How does nine o'clock sound?" Carson suggested. "I'm afraid I don't know which dorm is yours."

"They're in Mason Hall," Fly answered.

"That will work," the other girl sitting on the bunk said, flashing her beautiful green eyes at Carson.

After the girls left, Carson and Fly renewed their conversation.

"That girl with the green eyes is gorgeous, Fly. She was pretty quiet, though," Carson said.

"I can find out more about her if you want me to," Fly replied.

"I can do my own investigating," Carson said, laughing.

"Four girls and two guys is a little lopsided. Who else can we get to go with us?"

"I'll see if Sunny and a couple of the other cross-country guys from his dorm want to go with us."

Fly thought for a moment. "Hold on a minute, Carson. I can't go out on a date with you guys. What would I tell my girlfriend?"

"This isn't a date, Fly! It's a celebration. There just happen to be some girls tagging along. Besides, you didn't ask them, I did."

Minutes before the agreed-upon hour, Fly jumped into Carson's metalflake-green Dodge Demon. Carson turned the key, and the engine roared to life. He loved that car. He revved the 340-cubic-inch engine, feathering the gas pedal with his foot. It was equipped with special exhaust manifolds, a four-barrel carburetor, and a four-speed Hurst shifter. The torque was such that he could lay a patch of rubber with the oversize mag wheels in each of the first three gears if he wanted to show off. Tonight, however, he intended to be on his best behavior.

Carson asked Fly to call Mr. Trees on the CB radio. Fly enjoyed using his nickname as a CB handle but couldn't reach Mr. Trees. By the time they arrived at the girls' dorm, Sunny's compact car was already in the parking lot. He'd brought three cross-country runners with him. The four girls piled into Carson's vehicle. Three of them squeezed into the backseat, leaving the girl with the pretty green eyes to wedge herself between the two bucket seats occupied by Carson and Fly. Carson caught a whiff of her perfume, which immediately grabbed his attention.

"I never caught your name when you were in my room," Carson said.

"Paige," she replied, offering him a warm smile. "Bart, I mean Fly, mentions you a lot."

"Oh, really?" Carson replied, offering her a smile of his own.

"Where are we headed?" one of the girls sitting in back asked.

"Down the road a couple of miles to a place we call Ho Jo's," Carson replied. "Just so we are all on the same page, this is not a date. Fly here wants to have a clean conscience when he calls his girlfriend tonight."

Fly's cheeks reddened. Laughter and brutal teasing followed. Carson's announcement had broken the ice, and the conversation began to flow.

"Do you have any music you can play while we ride with you?" Paige asked.

"Push that cassette all the way in the tape player. I think it's Barbara Streisand's *Superman* album," Carson responded.

"How did you know Barbara Streisand was my favorite artist," Paige said excitedly as the title track, "Superman," began to play.

"I guess I just got lucky. I was really into the movie *Superman* when it came out last year, Carson said. "Paige, I have to use the gear shift, so I'll probably be bumping into your leg."

"I'll try not to hold it against you," Paige responded in a playful tone.

"Ho Jo's!" Fly shouted as they pulled into the restaurant. "I get it, only the H-o and J-o are lit up on the Howard Johnson sign."

"Great detective work, Sherlock," Carson said, laughing.

Carson led the group past the main counter, which featured a row of round chrome swiveling bar stools. His favorite spot was around the corner, an alcove near the restrooms. The small establishment was clean but couldn't hide the signs of its aging.

The girls were the first to pile into the U-shaped booth. They slid across the brown vinyl seats, leaving enough room for Carson and Fly to slide in on either side of them. Carson noticed Fly left the open spot next to Paige. Sunny, Shorty, and the two other runners arrived at the restaurant just as Carson's group was being seated.

They carried a table from across the aisle and pushed it against the round table. The runners sat in the wooden chairs they dragged over with the table.

"Sorry we're late. We got caught at a traffic light," Sunny said, flashing a smile.

Carson was happy to see they had this side of the restaurant to themselves. He didn't need the distraction of a rival group of students creating chaos by interfering in their conversation. The waitress took their orders, which included about as many different flavors of ice cream and milkshakes as there were people. The group had a lively conversation while they waited for their ice cream. The guys sitting at the table took great interest in the banter between the girls. Carson was no exception.

"Sunny, we missed you at Buffalo State yesterday," Fly said.

"I'm having problems with my knee. Coach said I should take the day off," Sunny replied. "Hey, Rookie, how'd you do yesterday?"

A puzzled look registered on the girls' faces.

"Who is Rookie?" one of the girls inquired, generating a round of laughter from the girls.

"Not bad," Carson answered. "I ran much better than the Geneseo meet."

Carson did not like having to own up to Sunny's nickname for him. He did his best not to show how irritated he was. Here he was trying to make a favorable impression on the girls, and Sunny was doing his best clown impersonation. Why had he invited him?

"You're the rookie?" Paige quietly asked, nudging him with her elbow. "I thought you were a senior."

"It's Sunny's attempt at humor," Carson replied.

"So, what do you think of our university so far?" Carson asked, changing the subject.

"It's sure different from high school," one of the girls answered.

"I like being away from my parents," another girl said.

"It's definitely a different feeling being on your own," Paige added.

"That's what I thought when I first got here, but this university really grows on you," Shorty said.

"Are you ready for freshman initiation?" Sunny asked, flashing a devious smile.

"What is that anyway?" one of the girls asked.

"Your beloved sophomore brothers and sisters have a plan to 'welcome' you into the student body. There's usually a little public humiliation involved. Everyone goes through it their freshman year. Sunny and I have nothing to do with it," Carson answered.

"Is anyone here a little homesick?" Fly asked.

A couple of heads nodded. The conversation continued until the last spoon clanked against the bottom of an empty glass dish. All ten students agreed to chip in to pay the bill after Carson's remark about this not being "a date." The girls insisted on riding back to the university together in Rookie's hot car. Sunny didn't try to hide his disappointment.

When they arrived back at the university, Fly got out of the passenger seat and slid the seat forward so the girls sitting in the back could get out. Paige and one of the other girls stuck their heads back in the car to thank Carson for the fun evening.

"Carson, this is one of my suitemates, Louise."

"Pleased to meet you," Carson replied. "Thanks for coming with us. I had fun."

Louise nudged Paige as if to encourage her to say something they had discussed earlier.

"Are you sure this wasn't a date, Carson?" Paige asked, offering him the warmest of smiles. "Fly told us you don't have a girlfriend."

"He did, did he?" Carson replied, trying not to laugh.

"Keep your eyes on that one," Carson overheard Louise telling Paige as the two girls walked away laughing.

Mr. Trees was back in the dorm when Carson returned. He looked up from the book he was studying when Carson entered the room.

"We tried to raise you on the CB earlier, but you didn't answer."

"I was studying with Clara."

"What were you studying?" Carson asked, kissing the air.

"I have a quiz tomorrow, if you must know," Mr. Trees replied. "Seems like I have an update for you, Shy Guy."

"What is it?"

"Clara told me the nursing students are going to nominate Lindsay Carter for homecoming queen."

"She's a quiet one. I'm happy for her. Are you sure she's up for it?"

"Apparently."

"But what's this got to do with me anyway?"

"Don't you remember? You agreed to be her escort!"

"That's not how I remember it," Carson said, laughing.

"You'd better go find Clara if you're not okay with it. They're going to make it official tomorrow."

Deep down Carson wasn't opposed to the idea. Lindsay was an attractive girl. How she remained unattached was a mystery to him because most of the cute senior girls already had boyfriends by the time they were seniors. Though he barely knew her, he was surprised that Lindsay was okay with him being her escort. He had a reputation on campus of being a rebel with a past. He guessed Clara was feeling sorry for him and wanted to set him up with a date. Brushing his apprehension aside, he embraced the possibility of escorting the next homecoming queen.

"Why were you trying to reach me earlier?" Mr. Trees asked.

"A bunch of us went out for ice cream, and we wanted to see if you and Clara wanted to join us."

"Who'd you go with?"

"Some freshman girls who visited us during the open house. I think they are friends of Fly. I invited some of the cross-country runners to join us."

"I see," Mr. Trees commented, pressing his fingertips together and leaning forward like a priest about to hear a confession.

"Stop it with the monsignor thing," Carson said, laughing. "We all agreed it wasn't a date, okay. I did think one of the girls was nice, though."

"Do tell."

"There isn't anything to tell other than she has a nice smile and pretty green eyes," Carson answered. "Sunny brought up the subject of freshman initiation. I think he was trying to scare the girls a little."

"Why would he bother with that? Seniors have nothing to do with initiation."

"But what if we wanted to have something to do with it?"

"Are you sure this doesn't have something to do with that freshman girl?"

"Her name is Paige, and I'd rather not say much more than that," Carson said, breaking into a smile. "Think big picture!"

"How big?"

"What if we could find out when initiation was and kidnap the entire freshman class?"

"Need I remind you that I'm an RA, and you shouldn't be telling me stuff like this. The university expects me to report troublemakers to the RD."

Mr. Trees's attempt at trying to stay in character was cut short when he could no longer keep a straight face. It took a few minutes for the laughter to die down. Carson really enjoyed their silly attempts at humor.

"For starters, I wouldn't use the word *kidnap* if you're planning to talk to anyone else about this," Mr. Trees said. "Kidnapping's a criminal offense."

"Okay. What if we hid the freshmen from the sophomores on initiation night, provided they were agreeable to it . . . theoretically speaking, of course."

"Where would we hide a hundred and fifty students?"

"Right here in the quad basement. We could throw a party."

"Well, Mr. Shy Guy, let me think about it."

"You always said you wanted to go out with a bang our senior year. This would make a really big bang."

CHAPTER SIX

onday's practice was different from any Carson had ever participated in. The team was preparing to face their rival, Houghton. Decades earlier it was commonplace for athletes from one institution to travel to the other institution and pull a prank just before a game. In response, the other university would find a way to retaliate.

Carson heard that one year the university's soccer team traveled to Houghton and hid their famous landmark, a big rock. Nobody could figure out how they could move such a heavy object. As it turned out, they never moved it. Someone came up with the idea of digging a large hole beside the rock, creating a massive pile of dirt over the rock, which hid the landmark. The rivalry had faded over the years, but the two schools usually drew a big crowd whenever they met.

Coach spent the day marking out the cross-country course using powdered chalk and signs. He assembled the team on the starting line and passed out stopwatches to the top five runners. Carson and his teammates were puzzled.

"Today we are going to try something a little different. I want you to work on establishing a consistent pace when you run. The purpose being to avoid a negative split. You shouldn't run the second half of the race faster than the first half. If you do, you put yourself in a position

"

of playing catch-up for the rest of the race." He paused, studying the runners.

"Judging from the confused looks on some of your faces, you'll have to trust me. It should be clear by the time we finish. We're going to start by running the first mile of the course. Then we'll stop and rest a few minutes. Those of you with stopwatches can check your time.

"Here's my philosophy. I want your first mile to be slightly faster than your normal pace. So, if you average five minutes and thirty seconds a mile, I want you to run the first mile fifteen seconds faster than you normally would."

Coach blew his whistle, and the team ran the first mile. The lead runners checked their stopwatches while everyone rested. Coach laid out his strategy for the second mile.

"By mile two you should be settling into your pace. Look for someone to run with. Try to avoid running by yourself."

He blew his whistle again. Carson ran with Shorty. After running the second mile of the course, they rested and checked their stopwatches again. Coach explained that the third mile was likely to be their slowest mile, especially if the course was hilly. He added that the seconds gained from the first mile were the cushion they would be using up here. The whistle blew again.

"Mile four is where the excitement begins. If you're running in a pack, watch for someone to try to break away. Be ready to go with them. If you manage to break away from a pack of runners, put enough distance between you and the other runners so that they lose contact with you. If you don't, they will catch back up with you. Finally, if you get passed by another runner, try to stay with him."

Another whistle, another mile.

"Mile five is the climax of the race. It's time to suck it up—refuse to lose," Coach said. "Every runner is hurting at this point. Draw on your training, remember how it made you sweat. Remember the pain you experienced. As you run, lift your knees high and push off with your toes. If you have another gear, use it. And don't let up when you reach the finish line. Run through it. You don't want to lose your finishing position at the last second."

Carson was intrigued by the amount of time Coach put into teaching them how to run the perfect race. He hoped that before the season ended, he would get a chance to experience such a race. When practice ended, Coach handed out their racing schedule. As Carson studied the schedule, one race leaped off the page. In a week's time, they would be traveling back to Geneseo. He found it odd that he wasn't dreading it; instead, he felt a fresh determination rise within him. He wasn't about to let the course beat him a second time.

On Wednesday, the team ran against Houghton. It was their first dual meet of the season. A dual meet is a race where one university competes directly against one other university, rather than multiple other teams. Dual meets made up the bulk of the university's schedule. The college newspaper said it was the first cross-country home win for the university in three years. Fly shattered the course record. Truman, Phantom, Einstein, and Spock also ran exceptionally well.

In cross-country a runner is awarded points based on their finish: one point for first, two points for second, etc. The scoring is limited to the first five runners on each team. All told, Carson's team captured the first five places, giving them the lowest possible score a team could receive: fifteen points. The team with the lowest score wins a cross-country race.

Carson crossed the finish line in ninth place with a time of 31:15, five minutes behind Fly. It was a measurable improvement over his previous finishes. Although he finished sixth on his own team, he and a teammate finished the race before Houghton's fifth runner. Carson saw firsthand the importance of being a team's sixth or seventh fastest runner. The more runners a team could get across the finish line before their opponent's top five runners, the more lopsided the score.

Hours after the race, Carson was left with an empty feeling. He wondered if it was because he didn't have a special someone to celebrate with. In that moment it surprised him that his thoughts turned to Paige. He had no reason to consider her as anything more than an acquaintance. But since the group outing to Ho Jo's, he had crossed paths with her several times. They acknowledged each other with a hello or a smile.

He couldn't pinpoint the day he started looking for her in crowds. But whenever he spotted her, it brightened his day. It forced him to consider that she did matter to him. Why then was he keeping his distance? He had no explanation for his inaction. Maybe it was because she was a freshman and he felt she deserved a chance to settle in to college life.

Two nights before his return to Geneseo, Carson had a vivid dream. He was walking through an endless wheat field. Each stalk waved gently in an almost nonexistent breeze. Feathery clouds danced across a deep blue sky as the sunlight fell on his shoulders. It was such a peaceful place. He was delighted to be there. So much so that he didn't want to leave.

He lingered in that place, drinking in the sun's warmth until it sank below the horizon. The sun left behind a rainbow of colors too beautiful to put into words. In that glorious moment, it occurred to him that he was alone. A cold chill raced up his spine from an unexpected gust of wind. He woke up startled. The empty feeling in his dream followed him back to reality. The hideous thought that hounded him had chased him down again: *One day you will leave this place and everything you hold dear, and you will find yourself alone.*

The next morning it took several hours for Carson to distance himself from the dream. He busied himself getting ready for the day and grabbed a quick breakfast before dashing off to his eight o'clock physics class. His day took a positive turn when he spotted Paige in between classes. She was in the basement of the music building where students picked up their mail.

Paige was wearing a soft pink sweater and a pair of black jeans that complimented her pleasant figure. Her curly brown hair fell gently on her shoulders. Her kind green eyes left the card she was reading and looked up at him. Carson froze when he realized she had caught him staring at her.

"Hi, Carson."

"Paige, it's good to see you."

"What brings you to the mailroom?"

"Just checking to see if I have any fan mail," Carson said, trying to recover.

"I didn't realize you were that popular."

"Sorry, I'm not. I was just trying to be funny."

Paige seemed to appreciate his attempt at humor.

Carson added, "Say, it's kind of short notice, but there's a movie playing on campus tomorrow night. Would you have any interest in going with me?"

"So would this be a date or another one of your nondates?" she asked.

"That depends on whether or not you have a boyfriend."

"I guess we'll have to call it a date then," she replied as a touch of color brightened her cheeks.

Carson could hardly contain his excitement as he walked with her up the stairs and out into the fresh air.

"I'll pick you up tomorrow night at six-thirty," he said before dashing off to his next class.

The following day Carson and Fly went for an afternoon run. Coach had given them the day off from practice because it was the day before the Geneseo meet. They kept their pace slow.

"Are you ready for Geneseo? It looked like that course really got to you last time," Fly offered.

"I think so. I've really improved over the last two races," Carson replied.

"On another note, I hear you're going to a movie tonight with Paige."

"How did you find that out? I haven't told anyone, not even my roommate."

"The girls in her dorm talk to each other, and sometimes they talk to me."

"I'll have to keep you in mind if I ever need a favor."

"You know I'd do anything for a friend."

Carson laughed. "What else do you know?"

Fly looked directly at Carson. "You won't be wasting your time getting to know Paige. She's a great girl. Louise and I can see that there's some chemistry between you two."

"I don't know what you're talking about," Carson said, smiling at his friend.

That evening as the sun was beginning to set, Carson and Paige walked to the science center to see the movie. Their stroll took them down through the center of campus. Paige remarked how she loved seeing the colors of the clouds as the sun was setting. Carson remembered the sunset in his dream. He smiled because now, in this scene, he wasn't alone. It was the first time Carson had been alone with her for any length of time, which might explain why he felt his pulse racing. He'd been on a number of dates over the past five years, but for some reason this one seemed different. When he considered Fly's comment about Paige being worth his time, it made his hands sweaty, so he stuffed them in his pockets.

"How was your day?" Carson asked.

"I've been pretty busy trying to keep up with all the reading and homework assignments," Paige answered. "My college classes are so much harder than high school."

"Nursing is a tough major. Students come here from all over the country because they have a great program."

"That's why I'm here."

"You know, I wanted to be a veterinarian when I was younger."

"Me too," Paige said, laughing.

"I guess we have something in common."

"How are you doing in cross-country? Fly tells me the team is off to a great start."

"I think I'm getting better every week. I'm not sure how long that trend will continue, but I'm going to enjoy it while it lasts."

"My father ran track in high school."

"That's interesting. Where are you from?"

"Binghamton, New York," Paige answered. "Fly tells me your family lives close to campus."

"Yes, I grew up about fifteen minutes from here. I tried to commute from home once, but I felt like I was missing out on too much of the campus life."

It was a little strange watching the movie in the same lecture hall where some of his classes were held. The room was patterned after an amphitheater. Students entered the room at the top level and descended a series of steps to find a seat. During classes, the lecturer stood at the bottom of the steps. Individual chairs ringed each level. Each chair had a foldaway table, which served as a writing surface. It was a bit too uncomfortable for Carson to sit through a two-hour movie, but he wasn't about to complain with a beautiful girl sitting beside him.

The movie was called *The Hiding Place*, a film about a Dutch family who hid Jews during the Second World War. The movie created an environment for Carson and Paige to talk about their faith as they walked together after the movie. Carson found it interesting that they were both in a similar place spiritually, learning to fully rely on God.

"Do you want to grab something to eat?" Carson asked.

"Can we check out the snack bar? I haven't eaten there yet," Paige replied.

"Perfect, I can check for any fan mail while we're there."

Paige grabbed Carson's upper arm with both hands and tugged on it. "You are such a guy,"

They had a good laugh before she let go.

"What is that supposed to mean?" Carson asked, thoroughly enjoying her banter.

"Men can be so full of themselves sometimes," Paige replied.

"Is that a nice way of saying that some men are self-centered?"

"Hey, you said it, I didn't."

They arrived at the music building, a large English Tudor structure that housed the music department on the top three floors. The mailroom, bookstore, and snack bar were in the basement of the building. They ordered milkshakes and grabbed a table in the back corner of the room. As they sipped on their shakes and talked, Carson saw several students he knew pass by. He watched some of their expressions change when they spotted Carson with Paige. One girl made a face at him when she passed. He was sure someone would start a rumor about the two of them later. The campus was so small that it was hard to keep a low profile, especially if you were trying to hide from someone or from something— like your past.

Carson discovered that he really enjoyed Paige's company. She was so easy to talk to. A kindness seemed to radiate from her being. Carson's heart sank when the student working behind the counter announced that the snack bar was closing.

"Do you want to check your mail before we go?" Carson asked.

"Are you asking for my benefit or yours?" Paige replied.

"What do you mean?"

"I thought you wanted to check your fan mail!" Paige said as the two of them walked over to the mailroom.

Neither of them had any mail. They walked side by side on one of the many asphalt sidewalks radiating out from the music building. When they reached her dorm, Carson wanted in the worst way to kiss her good night. In just the few hours he'd spent with her, she made him want to be the best version of himself. So he suppressed his desire to kiss her.

"I really had a great time tonight, Paige," Carson said, looking into her eyes.

"I did too," Paige replied, melting his heart with her beautiful green eyes.

Carson watched her retreat into the dorm, hoping she might reward him with one more glance. Just when he thought she wouldn't, Paige paused at the foot of the stairs and looked quickly back over her shoulder, offering him one last smile. She had plenty to talk about that night with her friend Louise.

Carson was disappointed that Mr. Trees wasn't in the room when he returned. His roommate had left a note on Carson's desk saying that he was asked to preach at his brother's church. He and Clara were gone for the weekend. Carson considered how great it was that his roommate was already stepping into his future. He laughed to himself when he imagined Mr. Trees trying to coerce a confession out of him regarding his date with Paige.

Carson climbed up into his bunk with his Bible and began leafing through it, trying to find a specific verse from the book of Isaiah. Eventually he found it.

"He gives power to the tired and worn out, and strength to the weak. Even the youths shall be exhausted, and young men will all give up. But they that wait upon the Lord shall renew their strength. They shall mount up with wings like eagles; they shall run and not be weary: they shall walk and not faint" (Isaiah 40:29–31). Carson studied the verses. He knew what it meant to be weak, exhausted, and ready to fall. He also believed that the Lord would give him strength if he called upon him, especially tomorrow in Geneseo. He buried the message in his heart and drifted off in a peaceful sleep.

CHAPTER SEVEN

Saturday morning Carson showered, shaved, and dressed, then headed to the dining hall for breakfast. But he had something besides the Geneseo meet on his mind. His heart radiated with warmth as he pondered his evening with Paige. He was lost in thought, ignoring the tray of food in front of him.

He thought about how much his life had changed since high school. Back then, he never went to any dances or proms. Girls intimidated him because he was self-conscious about his looks and was unsure of himself. The girls he did know were just friends.

When he arrived on campus as a freshman, all that changed. He was determined to get more involved with the girls he interacted with. He started asking them out, and to his surprise many of them said yes. His father was livid his sophomore year when he purchased a motorcycle on credit, but in Carson's mind it was worth it. Girls were constantly asking him for rides.

Carson enjoyed the fun and the romance girls offered. Before he knew it, dating had become a game to him. At the start of his junior year, he acquired his Dodge Demon. In his mind he had reached the mountaintop of his domain. That's when he started hearing this girl or that girl say he'd broken their heart after walking away from a relationship with them. It didn't take long before he could see how empty this lifestyle was. There was no future in it. After two particularly difficult breakups less than a year apart, the nice girls on campus started talking to one another, warning others to stay away from him. When he looked at himself in the mirror, he didn't like the person staring back at him.

By the end of his junior year the emptiness he felt in his life drove him to get serious about his relationship with Jesus Christ. Soon after, his attitude toward girls changed. He resolved if he was going to be involved with a girl, he wanted her to be someone God picked out for him. Carson wondered if this change was too late in coming.

"Good morning, Rookie. Everything okay?" Fly said.

"Yeah, I guess my mind is somewhere else," Carson answered.

"Are you worried about the Geneseo meet?"

"Actually, I was thinking about Paige."

"Is that all?" Fly said, laughing as he slapped Carson on the back.

"We had a great time. I'm trying to decide what I should do."

"I told you before, she's definitely worth your time."

"But what about *her* life. She's only been on campus for a couple of weeks."

"Have you forgotten that's how long I've been here, and thanks to you, I've adjusted very well. But then again, I'm not looking for a date."

"You should have seen the dirty look I got from one of the girls who saw us together. I'm glad Paige didn't see it."

"Do you really care about what someone else thinks?"

"No, I don't. Especially that one. I asked her out last year, and she turned me down," Carson responded, chuckling.

"Well, there you go. You have nothing to worry about."

"Fly, I'm a senior, and my time here is running out. Paige might be worth it, but I don't want to rush things and scare her off."

"You really are a rookie, aren't you? Don't you think she should have a say in what happens between the two of you?"

"Well, Doctor Fly, let's hope you run today as well as you give dating advice."

The two runners returned to the dorm and changed into their university-issued warm-ups. Carson felt clothed in nostalgia as he donned the ancient garments. These were the same ones worn by the state champions a decade ago. Carson and Fly jogged over to Sharpes Hall to join the rest of the team. When they arrived, Carson was surprised to see only three teammates sitting in the van.

"Where is the rest of the team?" Fly asked.

"Coach is checking the dorm to see if anyone else is coming," Spock replied.

"What about Truman?" Carson inquired.

"Murphy tore the toenail off his big toe horsing around in the dorm last night," Einstein said.

"Why did you call him Murphy?" Fly asked.

"Haven't you ever heard of Murphy's law? If something bad can happen, it's going to happen to Truman," Einstein replied.

The comment brought laughter, spoiling what should have been a solemn moment out of respect for one of the team's best runners on the team. The laughter stemmed from the absurdity of the situation. Truman had been injured twice already, and the season was young.

Coach returned to the van with more bad news.

"Shorty has the flu. The rest of your teammates are still nursing injuries. Thankfully, we still have five runners we can take to Geneseo. If another one of you goes down today, we'll have to forfeit."

Coach turned to Carson and said, "We need you today, Carson. You're our fifth man."

Spock, who was sitting in the seat behind him, slapped him on the back. Carson gave Coach a nod, too stunned to reply verbally. The weight of Coach's words rested heavily on his mind as they traveled to Geneseo. He had been preparing himself for something like this to happen, but he wasn't expecting it to happen so soon. He recalled the passage from the ninth chapter of Ecclesiastes when he first considered going out for cross-country. He hadn't committed it to memory but remembered the gist of it: The fastest runner doesn't always win the race; what matters is being in the right place at the right time.

Carson believed that God intervened in the affairs of men. His life was living proof. God had directed his path back to this university after he'd given up on college. He was surprised that the university had even allowed him to come back after his pitiful academic performance. But they did. Now he was watching God at work in his senior year. It's as if God knew the desires of his heart.

Cross-country was a perfect example. He shouldn't be performing as well as he was. The team's top runners spent the entire summer preparing, but his was a last-minute decision. Yet here he was being counted as one of them. As the events of the season began to unfold, Carson was catching a small glimpse of God's unfolding plan for his life. He wondered where this journey would take him. Carson believed he was in the right place at the right time.

The atmosphere in the van remained somber as they traveled through the beautiful Finger Lakes region. It was harvesting time for the local vineyards. Carson spotted workers and vehicles out in their fields gathering the fruits of their labor. Every person had a job to do, just like the cross-country team he belonged to. All five runners remained deep in thought as Coach drove.

When they arrived, Carson learned that this race counted as two dual meets. They would be racing against Fredonia and Geneseo simultaneously. Both universities were powerhouse teams with thousands of students. Coach thought it would be a good test, racing against two of the best teams in the area.

Carson was thankful that the weather remained ideal for a race. Even though the sun was bright in a cloudless blue sky, the temperature remained at sixty degrees. He felt a breeze, but it wasn't enough to cause a hindrance.

Although he dreaded the length of the race, Carson chose to focus on the elements he could control: his pace, his running form, and his nerves. The uphill climb was as taxing as he remembered it, but this time he avoided the mental strain that came from worrying about it. Carson was all business: taking short strides, leaning into the hill, and pumping his arms to power each stride. He also focused on his breathing, taking in deep breaths and expelling them slowly. He wanted to give his body a chance to absorb every ounce of oxygen carried by his red blood cells.

Since both teams they were racing against were top-ranked schools, Carson prepared himself for the likelihood that he would be one of the last runners to finish. He channeled all his energy into his primary responsibility: finishing the race.

Carson passed through the patch of woods and crossed the level grassy surface of the course at a steady pace. His legs recovered well from the uphill climb. He controlled his pace on the downhill portion of the race, holding back his speed slightly as the road snaked around the campus buildings. Eventually, the starting line came into view. The freshness of his stride surprised him as he began the second lap.

His second encounter with his climb up the hill brought pain. As the pain in his leg muscles continued to build, he offered a silent prayer. His breathing became labored. He thanked God for his health and waited on the Lord for renewed strength. He felt God strengthening his spirit and believed in his heart that he would not fail to finish the race despite the pain and exhaustion he felt.

He was credited with a twelfth-place finish in both meets with a time of 41:50. It was the first time Carson figured directly in the team's scoring, fulfilling one of the goals he'd set for himself. It was too bad it came as part of a losing effort. With the double loss, the university's dual meet record fell to one win and two losses. Coach, however, couldn't stop smiling.

"Carson, you just ran this course almost five minutes faster than you did eleven days ago. Who does something like that? Didn't I tell you that you'd see results soon?"

Carson's tired face brightened.

"I am proud of all you men for the effort you put in today," Coach said. "Yes, we got our butts whipped, but considering the adversity facing this team, no one should be hanging their head."

Fly passed by him grinning ear to ear, happy to see his friend succeed. Carson wondered how Fly could look that fresh after running such a brutal course.

"Hey, Rookie, nice work!" Spock said.

"You'd better watch out, Spock. I might just give you a run for your money before the end of the season," Carson replied.

"Let's not spoil the moment," Spock shot back, cackling.

Wednesday, four days later, the team faced Brockport State, a university ten times the size of Carson's school. Coach brought twelve runners to the meet, including Murphy, who was racing without a toenail. During the meet, Carson experienced another first—the first time he saw his performance dip. He ran the course on tired legs because he hadn't fully recovered from the Geneseo meet. He had a respectable time, 31:39, but finished in fourteenth place, seventh fastest on the team. Carson was unable to hide his disappointment.

"Rookie, don't let one bad race get to you. We've all had them," Spock said.

"You've got plenty of good races left in those legs," Einstein added.

"Thanks," Carson responded.

"Hey, Rookie, we won! Stop acting like we lost," Fly said.

"You know what? You're right, Fly," Carson replied, shaking off the setback.

The win evened their dual meet record at two wins and two losses. Carson chided himself later for losing sight of the fact that Fly had won the race and set a new course record.

≈

Lindsay Carter agreed to meet Carson in the dining hall for supper on Thursday to discuss the events surrounding homecoming next weekend. She was a beautiful twenty-one-year-old about four inches shorter than Carson. Her dark brown shoulder-length hair, brown eyes, and slender figure accentuated a kind face. Carson and Lindsay were an unlikely pairing. He had a reputation on campus of being a loverboy, while she maintained a quiet, bookish demeanor.

One of the things they discussed was a notice that arrived via campus mail notifying all the contestants that women competing for homecoming queen should wear dresses to the coronation event and the men should wear tuxedos. Carson had worn a tux only once before, and that was for his sister's wedding. He asked Clara if she would help him pick out a tuxedo. She arranged an outing for Lindsay and Carson to go Tuxedo Junction with her and Mr. Trees. There they picked out the perfect ensemble that would complement Lindsay's dress.

When Carson and Lindsay were spotted eating supper together for the second time in as many days, someone started a rumor that she was Carson's new girlfriend. The news spread over the campus like a brushfire driven by a stiff wind.

After supper Carson found Fly in the dorm, and the two of them went for a light run. Carson was learning that the more races he ran, the stiffer his leg muscles became afterward. Light workouts seemed to alleviate the stiffness without affecting his performance in the next race.

"What do you think of our home course?" Carson asked.

"It's fast, I like it," Fly replied.

"Might it have anything to do with the fact that you hold the course record?"

"Ha! What about you, do you like it?"

"Yes, in fact, I've set a new goal for myself. I think I can run this course in under thirty minutes."

"We both know you can do it," Fly said. "How do your legs feel today?"

"Not as tired as they did before the Brockport meet."

"Good," Fly replied. "Carson, there's something I have to tell you and you're not going to like it."

"About me or the course?"

"Neither. It's about Paige."

"What about her?"

"Sunny took Paige and her roommate out on a date last night. Shorty went with them."

"What?"

Carson stopped running and stared at Fly. What was he feeling? Was it anger, disappointment, jealousy, or perhaps betrayal?

"Why would he do that, Fly?"

"Well, you haven't really told anyone that you had your sights set on Paige."

"There's got to be more to it than that. A friend knows who his friend is interested in."

"Maybe Sunny heard the rumor that you and Lindsay are an item. It's all over campus."

"Yeah, and if I know Sunny, he probably started the rumor. It's not what people think, Fly. Lindsay is not interested in me or any other guy. She has a different plan for her life."

"Oh," Fly answered. "What are you going to do?"

"Homecoming is next week. If Lindsay is lucky, she'll be crowned homecoming queen. The least I can do is offer her my support."

Several hours later Carson was still stewing over Sunny's betrayal. He got into his Dodge Demon and closed the door. He sat in the dark and gripped the leather steering wheel. This car was a sanctuary for him, a place where he could think. He took comfort in the power and speed that enveloped him. The Demon had become a symbol of his success: a shy guy in high school labeled a misfit who had become a college student not afraid to take chances to get what he wanted.

But the past year had been a difficult one for him. He tried to involve God in the decisions he was making now. Some of those decisions still rubbed up against his past, and part of him still wanted to be popular with the girls on campus. Driving, like running, helped clear his head and put life back into perspective.

Carson started the engine and felt the seat vibrate from the more than three hundred horses hidden under the hood. He drove out of the parking lot aggressively, leaving behind a pair of tire streaks on the pavement. Gliding through the gears, he navigated his way to a familiar street near his parents' home. There was no posted speed limit on White

Road, but a yellow caution sign appeared as drivers approached a ninety-degree bend in the road. The recommended speed on the sign was twenty miles per hour.

The Demon sat on the road idling. Carson had raced at speeds exceeding 120 miles per hour, but this maneuver required skill not speed. His car lurched forward when he stomped on the gas pedal. He rapidly shifted through the gears, hoping that testing the limits of his car would somehow soothe the hurt he was feeling. It had worked for him in the past. Carson watched the speedometer climb: thirty . . . forty . . . fifty . . . fifty-five. The dangerous bend in the road approached rapidly. A small voice in his head whispered, *This is foolish.*

Carson took his foot off the gas and began pumping the brake aggressively. He fishtailed going into the bend, narrowly missing the guardrail. All four of Carson's limbs moved in concert—braking, clutching, shifting, and steering—attempting to bring the car back under control.

The Demon sat sideways in the middle of the road just past the ninety-degree bend. The smell of smoke from the overworked tires burned Carson's nostrils. The adrenaline rush he experienced had not cleared his head. At that moment he realized he had not completely let go of his past. He had let anger affect his behavior. His beloved Dodge Demon was a symbol of a past he could not let go of. He drove back to campus feeling ashamed that he had let God down.

CHAPTER EIGHT

eing a first-year cross-country runner meant that every course Carson visited was a new and different experience for him. The course at St. John Fisher was no exception. It lacked any familiar landmarks he could use to measure his progress. Carson and eight of his teammates used the time before the start of the race to loosen up. Coach informed the team that Murphy was lost for the season with a case of mononucleosis. The team let out a collective groan. Murphy's law had struck again.

Carson's girl troubles numbed him to his surroundings. He ignored Sunny when he passed by. When the starter's pistol fired, Carson thought it sounded strangely distant. With the race underway, he followed the bodies of the runners ahead of him, but his mind was elsewhere.

Why had he allowed himself to be talked into being Lindsay's escort? Was it because he was curious about her, or was it to appease Clara and her friends? He worried how Paige might react when she heard the rumor about him and Lindsay. Would she believe it? In the brief time he'd known Paige, she seemed to possess a maturity in her character that surpassed his own. It was one of the things he liked about her, which caused him to question his own personal growth over the past five years.

It bothered him that Sunny had taken an interest in Paige. Why? Carson could answer that question himself. She seemed like a beautiful person possessing a heart of gold. He felt betrayed by his friend and questioned his loyalty. Was Sunny using him just to get the girls he wanted?

The course he faced was straightforward, lacking hills or confusing turns. Runners were guided over roads, sidewalks, and grassy open spaces. It was flatter than his home course. Carson suddenly noticed he was having trouble controlling his breathing. Without realizing it, he had pressed his pace faster than he should have in the middle portion of the race.

When Carson reached the final stretch, the energy he counted on using to finish the race was not there. He'd already spent it. Unable to challenge any of the runners ahead of him, Carson coasted to a thirteenth-place finish overall and a disappointing sixth on his team. The team lost a close meet, and their record fell to two wins and three loses.

It wasn't until Carson checked his time, 31:01, that he realized how far he'd progressed. He'd shaved thirty-eight seconds off his time at the Brockport meet. This left him sixty-one seconds shy of breaking thirty minutes for a five-mile race. This truth was a tiny flicker of hope in the valley of darkness he found himself in.

⌦

Between his class schedule, his cross-country commitments, and the added stress of preparing for homecoming, Carson had little time for anything else. He did enjoy the brief time he got to spend with Lindsay, however. She was not as unapproachable as he guessed she'd be. He found her to be sweet and kind. But Lindsay was walking a different path, one that didn't involve dating or boyfriends. She had a specific plan for her future, one that included returning to South Africa after graduation to put her nursing degree to good use.

To her credit Lindsay maintained a laser focus, closing herself off from anyone or anything that would prevent her from doing so. Yet she had allowed herself to be nominated for homecoming queen, and an even greater mystery was why she'd agreed to let Carson be her escort.

Carson tried to concentrate on his daily routine, but he couldn't avoid the emptiness he felt inside. He tried to engage Paige when their paths crossed, but her response lacked the enthusiasm it once had. Something about her was different, and he needed to find out what it was.

❧

Carson pulled Fly aside after practice the day before their home meet against Hobart.

"Fly, can you to do me a favor?" Carson asked.

"Is this about Paige?" Fly answered.

"And how could you possibly know that?"

"Because it's written all over your face." Fly continued, "How can I help?"

"Paige isn't acting the same way toward me. Something is different. I've tried to be friendly, but she seems aloof, which for her seems impossible."

"Are you sure you'll to want to hear whatever I find out?"

"Fly, I don't have a claim on her, and I refuse to make any negative comments about her regardless of what you find out. She's a beautiful person and a fellow Christian."

"I wish more guys were like you, Carson."

"I'm not anyone you should pattern your life after. I'm just as flawed as the next person."

"Let me see what Paige has to say."

The next day Carson arrived on the field early and began his stretching routine. It was the first race in the month of October, and more importantly, they were more than halfway through the season. Nine of Carson's teammates were dressed for the race.

Carson approached the starting line nervous but excited. He needed his best effort in these last few races if he wanted to accomplish his goal. Hobart was a good team, but Coach insisted that they could be beaten.

Carson paid close attention to his pace for the first mile, pushing himself slightly faster than in previous races. He counted ten runners ahead of him; only four of them were teammates. Carson knew that the finishing order of the runners in front of him would determine who won the meet. His finish might also be a determining factor.

He continued to pace himself, suppressing a desire to run down the lead pack ahead of him. Shorty was running near him, so Carson urged him forward. Running together lessened the stress of the race for both runners. After three miles, Shorty was breathing harder than he would have wanted. Carson took a chance and left Shorty. He remembered that Coach cautioned them about intentionally running alone. A single runner was vulnerable to the runners behind him, and Carson knew Hobart had several.

Coach was standing at the four-mile mark and quickly briefed Carson as he ran past him.

"Hang on, Carson . . . It's the last mile . . . The score is close . . . Don't let anyone pass you."

Carson knew he was running in fifth position for the team. The pain in his legs grew as he pushed his pace faster. He was about to make the downhill plunge in front of the library, which meant he had less than a half mile to go.

"Hey, Rookie!" Shorty yelled from behind him. "They're coming for you!"

Carson glanced over his shoulder. Sure enough, three Hobart runners were grouped together and closing in fast. If they passed him, Carson believed his team would lose the meet for sure.

God, help me tolerate the pain, Carson prayed.

He could hear the labored breathing of one of the runners behind him. Ahead of him a crowd of supporters cheered from both sides of a roped-off area leading up to the finish line. He willed his body to move faster, and his lungs began to ache. He was out of breath. Then something unusual happened. Carson found the extra gear Coach once talked about. He heard other runners call it a kick.

A spiritual force inside him propelled him faster than he would normally be able to tolerate. He was using up oxygen at a faster rate than his body could produce it. Even as he gasped for breath, he forced himself to accelerate. Carson had gone anaerobic.

Somehow Carson managed to hold off three Hobart runners and finish in eleventh place. After crossing the finish line, he was so out of breath that he knew he was going to collapse. He quickly moved away from the crowd and slumped to the ground. He lay on his back, staring up at the sky as he struggled to breathe. He closed his eyes and felt a peace sweep over him. When he opened his eyes, he saw the familiar faces of Fly and Spock leaning over him.

"Are you okay?" Fly asked.

"I think so . . . How'd we do?" Carson said, raising himself up on his elbows.

"Rookie, that was an amazing finish! We beat Hobart!" Spock said, cackling.

"Don't make me laugh, Spock, my sides hurt," Carson replied. "What about my time?"

"Thirty forty-three," Fly said. "I know it's not what you wanted to hear, but you are getting closer every race."

"I'm coming for you, Spock. It won't be long now," Carson said, coughing as he tried to regain his normal breathing.

"You'd better rest awhile. You sound delusional," Spock replied. He tapped Carson on the knee and walked away.

After the crowd dispersed, Fly walked with Carson back to the dorm. Unbeknownst to Carson, Paige had watched his amazing finish from the library with a great deal of interest. Defeating Hobart evened their dual meet record again, making it three wins and three losses. Both men received congratulations from students as they walked through the center of campus in their uniforms.

"I don't know who had the bigger day," Fly said with a smile.

"You did, of course, because you won the race," Carson replied.

"Are you sure about that? As I recall, you were the one who held off three Hobart runners and saved the day."

"Were you able to find out anything about Paige?"

"Are you sure you want to talk about it now? It's not good, Carson. I've been waiting for the right time to tell you."

"How bad can it be? I haven't said or done anything wrong."

"She's been avoiding you, Carson. Apparently, Sunny has been supplying her with plenty of information about your past exploits with girls. The girl you broke up with last year was a friend of his. He also told her you're interested in Lindsay, not her."

"So he's ruining my already tarnished reputation and making me out to be a loverboy," Carson said. "Did you know the only reason Sunny went out for cross-country this season was to impress girls? That would explain why he's worked so hard against me."

"It's not all bad news, though. Because of the way Sunny trashed you, it pretty much cost him any chance with her."

"I don't understand. Paige and I seemed to be getting along so well."

"Honestly, I think she's taking a wait-and-see attitude. She's going to be guarding her heart around you, Carson."

"I guess some mistakes you never really stop paying for," Carson concluded.

"I did find out one positive thing. Her birthday is next week," Fly added. "But she won't be here for homecoming; she's going home to celebrate her birthday with her family."

Carson's heart was filled with an incredible sadness, and he reached out to God for mercy.

God, I've already confessed my past mistakes to you, and I know I've been forgiven. I'm turning over this situation with Paige to you because I don't know what else to do.

The university's cross-country team traveled back to the Finger Lakes region the following Wednesday to face Eisenhower College. The weather pattern had shifted dramatically in the past few days; a warm and sunny autumn had turned blustery and cold. After several days of rain, the sun was out, but the temperature had only reached fifty degrees. A steady wind chilled the air temperature further. Coach assessed the course as wet and muddy and cautioned the team to avoid any areas where water ponded on the surface.

Despite the cold weather and a wet course, the team notched another victory, improving their record to four wins and three losses. Fly just missed breaking another course record. Carson ran his best time of the season, albeit in waterlogged shoes. He finished the race ninth, fifth fastest on the team, with a time of 30:36.

On the trip home Carson pointed out to Spock that only forty seconds separated the two of them. Spock countered by reminding

Carson that everyone was entitled to one bad race. Spock's response had given their teammates a good laugh.

⚜

Two days later homecoming weekend began. All six contestants and their escorts were paraded up onto the platform during chapel on Friday morning. Based on the applause when Carson and Lindsay were introduced, he believed she stood a good chance of winning.

From the stage, Carson spotted Paige sitting in her assigned seat. She did not look happy when they made eye contact. Did he detect a twinge of jealousy, or was it something else? Whatever it was, it gave him cause for concern. He shook off the feeling that gripped his heart and waved to his fellow students as he stood beside Lindsay.

Throughout the day, students could vote for the candidate of their choice in the dining hall. The winner would be announced at eight o'clock that evening following a concert put on by the university's music department at the church adjacent to the campus. The event would be held in the church's fellowship hall, and a large crowd of alumni and students were expected to attend.

Carson refused to allow himself to stew over the news about Paige and Sunny. He was determined to make the best of his evening with Lindsay. The concert featured the university's traveling choir called the Chorale, whose performance was thoroughly enjoyed by the large crowd in attendance. Men in the choir were dressed in black tuxedos, while the women wore long black gowns, giving the evening a formal flair. When the moment came to coronate the homecoming queen, Carson found himself getting nervous for Lindsay.

The master of ceremonies began by announcing the candidates and their escorts. Polite applause followed each announcement. The contestants made their way up onto the stage after their names were called. Lindsay was one of the two candidates representing the senior class. Hers was the last name to be called. Carson escorted Lindsay to the stage in a light gray tuxedo. She wore a cream-colored full-length dress accentuated with white lace on the sleeves and collar. Carson thought she looked amazing. Her white-gloved hand rested on Carson's arm as they walked. When it came time to climb the steps leading up to the platform, he placed his free hand on hers to steady her.

A drawn-out moment of suspense followed as everyone in attendance waited for the MC to open the envelope and reveal the name of the winner. Carson's heart leaped for joy when he heard Lindsay's name announced. The crowd sprang to their feet and cheered. He was so happy for her. She humbly accepted the crown, which was accidentally placed upside down on her head. She cried as one of the officials placed a red robe over her shoulders and presented her with a bouquet of red roses. Laughter rippled through the crowd as the officials made a frantic scramble to flip the crown over on Lindsay's head. Carson was given a large vintage trophy to hold. Their names would be etched on it later to commemorate the event. Carson found the whole experience surreal.

A dessert reception followed the coronation. Lindsay and Carson posed for several pictures and were congratulated by a host of fellow students and alumni. Carson found it amusing that the only complaint logged by the students was that they weren't allowed to dance at the reception. Apparently, Christians shouldn't dance.

Once the reception was over, the crown, robe, and trophy were given back to the homecoming officials, and Carson suddenly felt awkward around Lindsay. Up until this point the two of them had a reason to be together. He was unsure how he should act around her now.

"Congratulations, Lindsay," Carson said, nervously giving her a hug.

"Thank you for keeping me upright. I was so nervous," Lindsay replied.

"I was nervous for you," Carson said, smiling.

Carson was the perfect gentleman and helped her into her coat.

"Would you like me to walk you back to your dorm?" Carson asked. "South Hall, right?"

"Yes. That would be nice, if you don't mind."

The conversation between them was sparse as they walked. He was pretty sure Lindsay felt as awkward as he did. The two of them paused briefly outside her dorm.

"It's been fun getting to know you, Lindsay. Thank you for giving me such a wonderful memory. Homecoming queen . . . wow!" Carson said nervously.

Lindsay stood for a moment and studied him. Carson wondered if she was reconsidering a vow she had made to herself. A few seconds passed and Carson began to feel a little uncomfortable. In the past he would have seized the opportunity and taken the initiative to kiss her good night, but he decided not to act because in that moment Carson's thoughts had turned to Paige. Lindsay sighed and offered him a polite smile. Then she leaned forward and kissed him softly on the cheek.

"Good night, Carson. Thank you for everything."

While there was a definite tone of gratitude in her words, Carson didn't detect the slightest hint of anything else. He walked across the courtyard to his dorm, relieved the whole experience was finally over.

CHAPTER NINE

Saturday morning a cross-country race was scheduled as part of the homecoming festivities. A large crowd was expected to attend given the team's rise from obscurity. The university was scheduled to host Buffalo State, who had already beaten them handily once this season. Carson played the course over in his mind, looking for a place he might be able to shave seconds off his time, but nothing stood out to him. He decided to seek Coach's advice.

Carson knocked on Coach's office door. "Do you have a minute?"

"What can I do for you, Carson?"

"I've been going over the course in my head, trying to figure out where I can shave about thirty seconds off my time. I'd like to run our home course in under thirty minutes before the season ends. At this point, I don't know if that's even possible."

"That's a pretty lofty goal this late in the season, considering that a lot of runners have already seen their times plateau."

"Why is that?"

"It's our racing schedule. When you race twice a week, your muscles start to fatigue. Your body doesn't have enough time in between races to fully recover, so the fatigue continues to build."

"I've been trying to keep my legs loose."

"I'm glad to hear that, because you're a prime candidate for muscle fatigue," Coach responded. "Haven't you been running at the top end of your capability since the very first day of practice?"

"You're right about that," Carson said, smiling. "So do you think I have a shot at it then?"

"I don't think you understand what I'm trying to tell you, Carson. Pressing harder at this point in the season will likely push you over the edge and lead to a muscle fatigue you won't be able to recover from until well into the off season. There is a limit to how much your body can take."

"What if I told you I'm willing to risk it?"

"What about the team? Are you willing to put their season at risk too?"

"Coach, I don't plan on letting anyone down, especially you."

"If you're dead set on doing this, you only have one option. That might not even be enough. You and I both know it's not a matter of running a little faster for the whole race. You're already racing at the top end of your ability."

Carson listened carefully. To his amazement, Coach had been watching his performance more closely than he realized.

Coach continued, "Remember the negative split I talked about at the beginning of the season? You've been running the second half of your races faster than the first half because you don't have the conditioning the other runners do. They developed their stamina over the summer. To find the seconds you're looking for, you'll need to start out a lot faster, which means your breathing will start to suffer earlier in the race. If you can't get your breathing under control, your race will be over after only a couple of miles. If you do manage to control your breathing, the stress you'll be putting your body through could put the rest of your season in jeopardy."

"What would you do if you were me?" Carson asked.

"I think you already know the answer. A champion won't settle for anything less than his best effort."

Carson thought about what Coach said as he walked back to his dorm. How much was he willing to risk? The team was down to seven runners. Sunny was the most recent casualty. His knees couldn't take the pounding cross-country runners had to endure. Carson had mixed feelings when he heard the news. Sunny was a friend, but he may have cost Carson a chance of getting to know Paige.

Since Carson was now running as the fifth man on the team, any personal gamble he made would likely affect the outcome of the race for the entire team. Increasing his speed for the first mile was not an easy proposition. Coach warned him about the dangers of doing it. If he was going to try this, there were two teammates he needed to talk to.

Carson and Fly arrived at the course and began their stretching routine.

"Fly, I'm going for thirty minutes today."

"That's the spirit!" Fly said. "Rookie, do me a favor and just don't do anything dumb that you'll regret later."

"By dumb do you mean starting out too fast?"

"Yes, I don't want you becoming a rabbit?"

"What's that supposed to mean?"

"A rabbit is a runner who starts too fast. They end up burning out after a mile or two. Opposing teams use rabbits as a weapon to sabotage the best runners on the other team. A runner can ruin his race by trying to chase down a rabbit."

"I can guarantee you I'm not a rabbit, but I am going to start faster than I normally do. I need to let Spock and Shorty know what's going on," Carson said.

"Well, Rookie, it sounds like you've got everything figured out. Good luck. Hopefully you'll make it to the finish line."

He found it ironic that for his plan to succeed he'd have to rely on two first-year runners, Spock and Shorty. He wanted Spock to help pace him for the first mile and Shorty to step in as the team's fifth runner if Carson faltered.

It was a cold morning. The weather was windy, and the sky was overcast. The temperature hovered near forty degrees, and with the wind factored in it felt closer to thirty. It was just one more thing Carson had to overcome to reach his goal.

The course was designed to start, and finish, near the tennis courts. The Buffalo State runners were out on the course trying to make sense of the map Coach gave them.

Spock and Shorty both said they understood what Carson was trying to accomplish, although Spock thought he was crazy for trying such a thing. Carson felt bad for Shorty because he was asking him to carry an extra burden during the race.

Carson was a bundle of nerves as stood beside Spock waiting for the starting gun to sound. His nervous energy was immediately converted into explosive motion as the runners left the starting line. Spock's opening pace was definitely faster than Carson was used to, but he stayed with him.

From the starting line, the course ran north behind two baseball fields until they encountered the cinder track where they would make two laps before continuing east. A solid chalk line guided the runners from there on, throughout the entire course.

"How are you holding up?" Spock asked.

"This is way faster than I'm used to, but my legs are doing fine," Carson answered.

"Rookie, your breathing is giving you away. You're pushing too hard. It's only been three quarters of a mile, and you're practically gasping for breath. You'd better back off before you go anaerobic."

"You're probably right, Spock. Thanks for getting me started."

Carson returned to a pace he was used to running. Fortunately, they were in one of the flat portions of the course. His immediate priority was to get his breathing back under control. If he couldn't, his race was over. He chased away a twinge of panic that prophesied his doom.

God, I know you put me on this team for a reason. You have plans for me to prosper, not to see me fail. Calm my spirit. My hope rests solely in you. It's your breath in my lungs. It's your breath in my lungs . . .

Carson repeated the last sentence of his prayer over and over in his mind. He continued along the solid chalk line for another three quarters of a mile as it snaked around a huge open field. Carson approached a small signpost standing in the middle of the field. It was a critical junction point in the course because runners visited it three times during the race: first encounter, turn right; second, go straight; and third, turn left. Opposing runners who didn't take the time to study the course could easily be confused by it.

Carson turned right at the signpost, following the chalk line, which made a wide arc before approaching one of the few hills on the course. The base of the hill marked the two-mile mark on the course. He pushed himself up the hill and past a handful of campus buildings.

From there he followed a portion of Vine Street down to Townline Drive. His body was getting tired. Even the slightest change in elevation affected his breathing. He left the road and headed due south once again across the expansive field he'd encountered earlier. He ran straight past the signpost and headed for Main Street. The road portion of the course required him to run up a slight incline on Main and face a steep uphill climb on Vine Street. That hill all but robbed him of his breath.

He ran down through the center of campus and a length of Townline Drive, where they entered the great field again. He approached the signpost for the last time before turning left and heading back through the center of campus. He pushed hard over the final stretch course but lacked the energy for an amazing finish.

Carson scored an eleventh-place finish, fifth fastest on the team, against an incredibly strong Buffalo State team. Even though they lost to Buffalo, they were awarded a win against Daemon College who never showed up. Their dual meet record stood at five wins and four losses with one more dual meet left in the season. If they won that meet, the university would be assured of a winning record for the first time in nine years.

Carson had his best finishing time of the season, 30:18, slashing eighteen seconds off his previous time. The pain in his legs didn't immediately leave him after the race. Carson knew he was bumping up against muscle fatigue and was playing with fire by pushing himself hard this late in the season.

After the race, Carson remembered there was something he needed to take care of. Ten minutes later, he stood in the town drugstore rifling through a large display of greeting cards. After about thirty minutes of browsing, he found the perfect birthday card. It had an image he liked and a verse that closely resembled his sentiments. Carson signed the card "A friend" and placed it in campus mail.

Over the weekend, a second rumor started. This one said Carson dumped Lindsay because she wouldn't go out with him. Fly continued to be an excellent source of information. Carson was tired of people portraying him in such a bad light. Didn't they realize he was committed to being a better person.

Carson and Mr. Trees ate lunch together on Monday while Clara was away at clinical training.

"What happened between you and Lindsay?" Mr. Trees asked.

"Nothing. She doesn't want any guys in her life right now. She wants to return to South Africa after graduation," Carson answered.

"It's all over campus that you dumped her, or she dumped you, depending on who you talk to."

"I'm tired of all the gossip. Don't you think I'm a different person now?"

"Yes, I know you are," Mr. Trees answered.

They sat in silence for a few minutes. Carson smiled as he reminisced about how the two of them had forged a friendship during the days of their fun rebellion, doing things they weren't supposed to just because it was fun. Those days seemed so long ago. A sadness washed over Carson when he realized how much he'd miss Mr. Trees and Clara after graduation.

"We need to do something fun to cheer you up!" Mr. Trees announced.

"What did you have in mind?"

"Why don't we go out prowling tonight."

Carson thought about it for a moment.

"How about a car race instead?"

"I'm not racing your Demon. You forget that I have a Vega. It wouldn't even be a race."

"I thought you wanted to cheer me up," Carson said, laughing. "Okay, how about if I make it even. Your yellow Chevy Vega against my parents' yellow Ford Pinto."

"I'm listening," Mr. Trees said with a smile. "Where would this race take place, Mario Andretti?"

"How about on the cinder track the runners use?"

"Shy Guy, sometimes you come up with the best ideas."

After practice Carson went home to ask his mother if he could borrow her car for what he called a "campus event." She was more than happy to lend it to him because she was proud of her scholarly son. He was going to be the first person in the family to get a four-year college degree.

Her Pinto was a subcompact car equipped with a four-cylinder engine, making it comparable to Mr. Trees's car. But it had less than one quarter of the horsepower that his Dodge Demon possessed. Mr. Trees met him in the library after supper to discuss the race.

It was a busy evening, and the library was being heavily used. Carson and Mr. Trees found a table on the lower level where they were less likely to be "shushed" by the head librarian on duty. Carson chuckled to himself as he peered out of one of the large plate glass windows overlooking the track.

What a perfect view for our stunt, he thought.

"It's eight thirty. Are we still going to do this?" Mr. Trees asked.

"I'm game. If we wait any longer, we'll risk being caught," Carson replied.

"Look at all these people!" Mr. Trees whispered. "Go over the plan one more time so we don't crash into each other."

"That's probably a good idea," Carson affirmed. "You follow me down through the center of campus past the library. Two bright yellow vehicles ought to draw a lot of attention. I'll turn off onto the lawn before we get to Townline Drive. Follow me around the base of the hill past the library and onto the track. Two laps around the track ought to do it. Not too fast, okay. I don't want to have to pay for property damage. We'll leave the same way we came."

"I think this will be fun," Mr. Trees said out loud, unable to contain himself.

"Shh!" Carson said, trying hard not to laugh.

The mid-October night was warm, which meant there wasn't much dew on the grass. They drove across the lawn without damaging it or leaving ruts. Carson's Pinto sat on the track, waiting for Mr. Trees to pull up beside him. This wasn't going to be a race in the real sense, but they wanted to make it look like one.

Mr. Trees pulled up alongside Carson, and the two of them revved their engines. Carson knew the clock was ticking and campus security could intervene at any moment.

The two drivers remained side by side as best they could for the first lap. He let Mr. Trees have the inside lane, and he took the outside. Halfway through the second lap Carson picked up speed and took the lead as they continued to race but now in single file. Carson smiled when he noticed that every window in the library was occupied by students watching their shenanigans. He left the track and made a break for Townline Drive. His heart didn't stop racing until he was almost home.

Carson told his mother he had participated in a kind of road rally but he didn't win. He realized he was stretching the truth, but it was the only way to keep her from asking a dozen more questions.

The next day Carson and Mr. Trees attended their classes, acting like the race never happened. For Carson, the hardest part was keeping a straight face when the students around him were buzzing about their crazy stunt. Evidently, a lot of people saw it happen, and even more wished they had, including a beat writer for the university's newspaper. After a blurb appeared in the campus paper vowing to determine the identity of the two drivers, Mr. Trees knew it was only a matter of time before his yellow car was implicated. When he was confronted by a reporter about the incident later, Mr. Trees was quoted as saying, "Hey, you guys are trying to get me in trouble."

CHAPTER TEN

Carson loved fall. It was his favorite time of year. He loved walking among the mature maple and oak trees dominating the campus grounds. Their colorful leaves gave the landscape a timeless, romantic air. He and his fellow students didn't mind shuffling through the fallen leaves as they moved between classes.

It bothered Carson that he hadn't been able to learn when the sophomores would hold initiation. He witnessed how the delay brought a sense of dread to freshman students whose minds were fed a steady diet of folklore by upperclassmen. Both he and Mr. Trees continued to make inquiries, but the date remained a closely guarded secret.

Several of his friends, including Fly, Spock, and Paige, were freshmen. He was determined to intercede on their behalf if humanly possible. Carson recalled his own college initiation experience, being awakened at three o'clock in the morning by a trumpeter roaming the hallway. He was dragged out of bed, told to dress quickly, and herded into the dining hall along with the other freshmen from his dorm.

Once in the dining hall, he was taught a song and had to rehearse the accompanying choreography. His outfit was dictated to him as well. "Wear a pair of shorts over your clothes today, and carry an umbrella if you know what's good for you," they told him. He was given a childish red-and-white beanie, which he was instructed to wear at all times.

The umbrella proved useful, warding off water as it was poured from a glass above him while he performed the song-and-dance routine. It was perhaps the most humiliating day he'd ever experienced as a college student. Those who refused to comply with the ritual were subjected to even more humiliation in a kangaroo court held later that night.

At supper Tuesday evening Fly seemed restless and fidgety. It was so unlike him.

"What's bothering you?" Carson asked.

"We have our first championship meet tomorrow," Fly replied. "I guess I'm just nervous."

"I've never seen you nervous before a race," Carson said with a laugh. "What's going on?"

"Maybe I'm nervous for you. Humor me and go for a run with me."

"It's almost dark. Are you sure you want to do this?"

Fly's suggestion was a bit unusual since they'd finished cross-country practice a few hours earlier. Carson thought maybe if he went with Fly, he could get to the bottom of whatever was bothering him. As they ran, the footing grew more treacherous with the darkening sky. Carson was worried one of them might twist an ankle.

"I don't think this is a good idea," Carson said. "Coach won't be happy if one of us gets hurt."

"Let's head for the track. We can finish up there," Fly said, sporting a devious smile.

"Is there something you want to tell me? If so, come right out and say it."

"Look, I see girls jogging on the track," Fly said, ignoring his friend's inquiry.

"I wonder what they're doing here after dark?" Carson countered.

"I don't believe it. Carson, I think that's Paige in the red sweats."

Carson wasted no time debating Fly as to whether or not it was Paige. He needed to find out for himself and bolted down onto the cinder track. Fly stopped to admire his accomplishment.

"Hi Paige, what are you doing here?" Carson asked, slowing his pace to match hers.

"I thought I could use a study break," Paige replied.

"I didn't know you ran."

"Ha, I wouldn't call this running."

"Do you have a few minutes to talk?"

"Okay, sure," Paige said, as she waved off Fly behind her back.

"Maybe we should sit down first. It sounds like you're out of breath."

"That's probably a good idea."

Carson glanced up at the stars as they walked toward the bleachers. God's handiwork was on full display in the dark sky. A lone streetlight guided them to a spot on the bottom bench. He brushed aside flecks of peeling green paint before they sat down.

Surrounded by darkness, a single beam of light fell gently on her form. Carson thought Paige looked amazing in her red sweats. He loved the way loose strands of hair fell across her face, giving her features a playful charm. This was his chance to plead his case with the girl whose spirit and beauty challenged his very being in ways he never thought possible. It was a moment in time he wanted to cherish forever.

The gravity of the moment made him extremely nervous. There were so many things he wanted to say to her. A host of thoughts swirled in his head and suddenly ran together in a jumbled mess, causing him to stumble over his words.

"I, um, well, I'd like to . . ." Carson faltered.

"What is it, Carson?" Paige interrupted. "Talk to me."

Carson paused. He took a deep breath and waited for the merry-go-round of words to stop whirling in his head.

"I'd like to see you again, but I don't know how things stand between you and Sunny."

"Fly said you might want to talk to me about that."

"Speaking of Fly, where is he?" Carson asked, looking around. "Your friends seemed to have vanished as well."

"I guess they had somewhere else to be," Paige said, trying to suppress a smile.

"So I've been set up," Carson said, smiling.

"You certainly catch on quick; I'll give you that."

"I heard through the grapevine that Sunny told you some things about me, and I wanted to give you a chance to talk about whatever he told you. You can ask me anything, and I'll be truthful with you."

"Is it true that you broke up with that girl last year? Sunny said you hurt her bad."

"Boy, you don't waste any time beating around the bush, do you?" Carson said. "Yes, that's true."

Here we go, God. You gave me this opportunity. Please help me know what to say.

"Paige, it's important that you understand that I'm not the same person I was a year ago. Still, I can't change what happened. There's no excuse for the way I treated her. I was selfish and didn't consider her feelings. She said that I used her, and that's probably truer than I'd care to admit. But what Sunny probably didn't tell you is that I owned up to my mistake. I spent time talking to her and went out of my way to make sure she was okay. I think we ultimately parted on good terms."

"So you're not the cruel and heartless person some people say you are?" Paige replied.

"Look, Paige, I'm no saint. But people like Sunny shouldn't say things they have no business saying. I don't know what Sunny's motive was. He's supposed to be my friend."

"What about Lindsay? I heard a rumor that you broke things off with her after homecoming."

"Paige, you can't believe everything you hear on this campus."

Carson's heart was on the verge of breaking. Was he watching himself lose the battle to gain the trust of one person who mattered the most to him? How could he prove to Paige that she could trust him?

"Here's the truth," Carson said. "It's up to you whether you want to believe me or not. From what I could tell, Lindsay wanted something to remember her college experience by, and for her that meant running for homecoming queen. I am happy it worked out for her. I was simply trying to be a nice guy and help her out. I allowed myself to be roped in to being her escort. Lindsay is a kind and sweet person, but she was never looking for a boyfriend. She has other plans for her life that don't include being involved in a relationship right now. Believe it or not, she plans to return to South Africa after graduation."

"I guess that explains a lot . . . and congratulations on winning, by the way. I certainly can't fault you for wanting to help someone realize a dream. Would you do something like that for me?"

"Of course, because I care about you."

"I saw pictures of you in your tuxedo. You looked very handsome. You're sure to get some fan mail now from girls wanting to go out with you."

"I'm only interested in one girl," Carson replied as he looked directly at Paige.

He noticed Paige looking intently into his eyes. He hoped she could tell there was no deceit in them. He was being as honest as he could. What would it take to break through her defenses? Carson noticed her countenance had changed. She was no longer interrogating him. The hardened features of her face were softening. He looked at her with eyes that could love and cherish her if she could only believe him. How could he convince her that she could trust him?

Carson continued. "I'm looking for a friend, Paige. Someone I can talk to about anything. Someone who inspires me to love them more than I love myself. A person I hold in such high regard that she inspires me to be a better person. If you ever hear of someone like that, be sure to drop me a note in the mail."

When he finished talking, the silence was deafening.

"So, everything Fly has been telling me about you has been true," Paige said, as if thinking out loud.

"I don't know what he told you, but I can tell you that what you think about me matters," Carson said, feeling tears pooling in his eyes.

"You wouldn't happen to know who sent me an anonymous birthday card in campus mail the other day, would you?" Paige asked.

She leaned her shoulder into Carson's side before pulling away. Her brief contact with him made his senses tingle. Carson noticed tears forming in Paige's eyes for the first time since he'd known her.

"You mean the one with the picture of the cottage by the lake? I bet that guy really wants to be your friend," he replied, smiling as he dried his eyes.

"So it was you," Paige answered, as if trying to bring her emotions back under control.

"You never answered my question about you and Sunny," Carson said.

"You don't need to worry about him anymore," Paige answered. "Carson, look at me."

She grabbed Carson's chin with both hands and turned his face toward her. Her hands were trembling.

"You need to impress me and no one else," she said.

Carson saw that the warmth had returned to her smile and the kindness to her eyes. No matter what else happened between them, he knew that she knew the truth about him. It was up to her to decide what, if anything, she intended to do about it.

Carson watched Paige's cheeks flush. Her eyes suddenly carried a hint of panic. It looked to Carson like she was coming undone right in front of him.

"Carson, I need to get back to the dorm."

"Let me walk you back," Carson responded, noticing that his hands were sweaty.

As they stood to walk home, Paige said, "I saw the end of your cross-country race last week. I was watching from the library."

"So, you *are* interested in cross-country," Carson replied.

"Hey, a couple of my friends happen to be on the team."

"Friends. Hmm, that narrows it down quite a bit since there's only seven of us left."

"I've been watching this one guy . . . I think they call him Rookie."

Paige left Carson standing outside her dorm. Once again, she had found a way to gain the upper hand, but he didn't mind. Her playfulness was one of the things he liked about her. He had risked his future with her tonight. Telling the truth was supposed to hurt, but somehow his heart felt liberated from a burden in his past. Carson walked back to his dorm. He couldn't say for sure whether his feet were actually touching the ground. Hope radiated from his soul, and he took a moment to be thankful.

God, I've been searching for someone like her my whole life. But you know me better than I know myself. Do I have the capacity to love someone like Paige? She deserves to be loved and cherished. Thank you for helping me say what I needed to say tonight. I am so undeserving of your mercy.

When Carson entered his dorm room, his roommate was grinning from ear to ear.

"Where have you been? I've got some good news," Mr. Trees said.

"Good news? Well, that seems to be the theme tonight," Carson replied.

"What do you mean by that?"

"I finally got a chance to talk to someone I've been wanting to talk to for a while."

"Knowing you, that had to be a girl."

"You're right about that," Carson replied. "I'm sorry, you said you had some good news."

"Carson, initiation is Thursday night," Mr. Trees announced.

"Today is Tuesday, that doesn't give us much time," Carson replied. "How did you find out?"

"Clara heard it from one of her nursing friends. She says the information is reliable because it came from the RD's wife via the dean of students. That poor women let it slip out in a conversation."

"Wow, how did we ever get so lucky?" Carson said. "What do you want to do?"

"I say we should give your plan a try, but we need be careful who we tell. I don't want Clara getting into trouble," Mr. Trees replied.

"Sounds like we're hosting a party then. I'll see if Renee can help us. Without her help there's no point in trying. You and I aren't going to entertain a hundred freshman girls by ourselves. I'll talk to Renee after class tomorrow."

"Mason Hall is where most of the freshman girls are. Maybe Clara can find someone willing to help us."

"I wish we had more time to figure out how to get the freshman guys out of Sharpes Hall."

"We'd better just focus on the girls' dorms."

"Let's hope we don't get kicked out of school for doing this," Carson said, slapping Mr. Trees on the back.

"Yeah, I don't imagine that would look very good on a pastor's résumé," Mr. Trees replied.

CHAPTER ELEVEN

Carson left his roommate a note Wednesday after lunch before leaving for his cross-country meet at Houghton: "Mr. Trees, let's get together tonight at 8:00 in the library to plan our strategy. Hopefully, we have enough players for the game. Shy Guy"

Houghton was an hour drive south from the university. It was the first of three championship meets the team was scheduled to compete in. Each year a different college hosted the Private College Athletic Conference, or PCAC, championship. This year it was Houghton's turn. The university would compete against three other teams for the trophy. They had faced all of them at least once this season, and St. John Fisher College remained the team to beat.

Coach warned them that this was likely one of the toughest courses they would run all season, largely because Houghton had a beginner's ski slope on campus. Still, Carson was brimming with confidence, having improved his finishing times the last several meets. The weather proved favorable, a comfortable fifty-five degrees, and the sky was overcast.

The opening miles of the course were surprisingly easy. Carson ran across two athletic fields and followed the course as it transitioned onto a highway. Just when he began to relax, the runners in front of him turned off the road and began their assault on a hill. It was the most brutal ascent Carson had ever been exposed to. A rolling trail rose steadily for over a mile. In Carson's mind the grade of this hill was worse than the one he'd encountered in Geneseo. The ascent cost him huge chunks of both time and energy—energy he needed to finish the race. But he was not alone; runners all around him were laboring. Eventually, Carson finished his ascent.

When he reached the summit, he caught a breathtaking glimpse of the college and the surrounding landscape. But the experience was short-lived when he noticed a sign directing runners to the ski slope. A rugged descent followed. His knee and hip joints ached from absorbing repeated jolts from the weight of his body as the ground fell away beneath his feet. Halfway down the slope Carson could see runners ahead of him on the course below. From his vantage point there was nothing but athletic fields remaining.

Thank you, God, for helping me on this course. I am grateful, Carson prayed as he forged on.

With four teams competing, every runner who finished in the top ten could dramatically improve his team's chances of winning the event. Fly finished first, and a runner from Eisenhower finished second. St. John Fisher won the meet because all five of their runners finished in fifth through ninth place. Their total score was thirty-five points, lowest of all the teams competing.

Carson was happy to see that his university finished in second place, beating out Eisenhower and Houghton. He personally managed an eighteenth-place finish overall, scoring fifth for the team with a time of 31:49. Carson judged his finishing time as a colossal failure, a ninety-one-second setback over his previous race.

After congratulating his teammates and celebrating their second-place finish, Carson kept to himself on the ride home. What happened to him today? He couldn't come up with an excuse other than blaming his setback on the difficulty of the course. He wondered if he was still capable of finishing a five-mile course in under thirty minutes. Coach had warned him about the possibility of muscle fatigue setting in. He took solace in the fact that he still had a full week to get ready for their last home meet.

⚍

Carson caught up with Renee, Clara, Mr. Trees, and Susan (an RA Clara had recruited from Mason Hall) later that night in the library. To his knowledge no one had ever attempted what they were about to do. He wondered, if he had an extra week to ponder this stunt, would he still go through with it?

"Susan, we are grateful that you want to help us," Clara said. "My boyfriend and Carson here think they can pull off this crazy scheme."

"I hated initiation. I always thought it was childish. So how can I help?" Susan asked.

"We need to keep this simple; otherwise, we are liable to get caught and find ourselves in a lot of trouble. I think it's pretty much a given that we should focus exclusively on the freshman girls in Mason and Omega," Carson offered. "With that many girls missing from their dorms, it's going to throw a wrench into the initiation proceedings."

"My roommate and a couple of trusted friends are prepared to welcome the girls to North Hall. We're going to host a party for them in the basement. It's a big enough space and it's hidden from view," Renee said. "So how do we plan on moving the ladies?"

"Mr. Trees and I should be able to escort them in small groups. For Mason that's probably one floor at a time. Is that something you can manage?" Carson asked Susan.

"I should be able to," she answered. "Unfortunately, I'll be working by myself because the other RA went home for the weekend."

"We think Mason should be the first dorm we tackle because it's the closest building to ours. Omega is on the other side of campus and could present a challenge," Carson added.

"I think there may be something like ten freshman girls staying in Omega. I can help you escort them," Clara said.

"I'm planning on going to Omega once we're done with Mason," Mr. Trees added.

"What exactly are we going to tell the girls?" Renee asked.

"I think we should be honest with them. Tell them that initiation starts in a matter of hours, and we're offering them a chance to get a little extra sleep and escape some of the drama. Tell them they're invited to a party hosted by North Hall," Carson replied. "We've all been through initiation. I know I would have skipped it for a party."

"You know, this is beginning to sound like a slumber party," Mr. Trees countered.

"If it's a slumber party, they're going to need bedding," Renee added.

"What if we tell them to bring a pillow and a blanket?" Susan proposed.

"I like that idea," Clara replied.

"Renee, can you station somebody in the lobby to let us in the building once we get there? The doors are going to be locked," Carson offered.

"That's not a problem," Renee responded.

"If it's a slumber party, Mr. Trees and I won't be attending," Carson said, laughing. "We'll stay upstairs and guard the lobby in case a sophomore comes looking for the girls. I'll babysit the front door while

Mr. Trees goes to get Clara and the Omega girls. Once everyone is here, we'll keep an eye out for the night watchman. He'll be coming through at some point. When he does, Mr. Trees and I will create a diversion and lure him away from North Hall."

"We've certainly had plenty of practice doing that," Mr. Trees said, chuckling.

"Should we tell the RDs in North Hall and Mason what we are up to?" Clara asked.

The RD in North Hall lived in an apartment directly above where all the students would be gathering. Likewise, the girls would have to pass by an RD's apartment on their way out of Mason.

"What if they tell us we can't do it?" Mr. Trees said.

"I guess it's a no then. We'll have to play that one by ear," Carson said. "Remember we're not harming anyone, and we certainly don't want to harbor any girl against her will. I think we could argue that the girls are not breaking curfew because they will be inside the dorm after hours, even if they are in the basement."

"I think most of the girls in Mason will want to come," Susan said. "At this point they're fed up with all the stories floating around about how terrible initiation is going to be."

"That's what we're counting on," Mr. Trees replied.

Twenty-seven hours later, at the stroke of midnight, Mr. Trees and Carson brought the first group of girls from Mason Hall to North Hall. They were aided by a new moon, which darkened the night sky, covering their movement like a blanket.

Renee opened the locked entry door for Carson and the girls when they arrived. She led them down a flight of stairs and into the brightly lit basement. The smell of popcorn hung in the air while a color television played *The Tonight Show*. Two of Renee's trusted friends served as hostesses and got the girls settled in. Renee put herself in charge of filling rows of plastic cups with water and soda.

Susan had perhaps the most difficult task of anyone involved in the plot. She had to explain the plan to dozens of girls at a time and keep them quiet so as not to arouse suspicion. She was hard at work getting the girls on the second floor ready when she realized there was one suite of sophomore girls on that floor. She thought it odd that they had gone to bed early, but it made perfect sense now as she thought about it. They were probably involved in the initiation proceedings. Susan was careful not to disturb them.

Carson and Mr. Trees waited behind a row of shrubs for Susan to appear in the lobby with the second group of girls.

"So far, so good," Carson said.

"Let's hope you didn't just jinx us," Mr. Trees replied.

"I thought you were going to be a minister. Should you be using words like *jinx*?"

"You're not a theologian, so how would you know?" Mr. Trees shot back. "Besides, I'm not ordained yet."

Carson laughed at his response. "Here come the girls. Let's go."

Susan had managed to get two floors of girls past the RD's apartment without arousing suspicion. Carson hoped their luck would continue. They led the girls from the second floor to North Hall, where a spotter placed by Renee let them in. Carson and Mr. Trees grew concerned when they realized their plan was taking longer to execute than they envisioned. They still had more than half the girls to transport.

"We need to find out where the night watchman is before we get another group," Mr. Trees said.

"Why don't you go wait outside Mason, and I'll go look for Walter? Don't move the girls until I join you, okay?" Carson replied.

After five minutes of looking without success, Carson gave up and went to look for his roommate. Mr. Trees was hiding behind the same row of shrubs. When Carson walked out into the open, Mr. Trees frantically signaled for him to get down and be quiet. Carson dropped to the ground and froze.

The girls from the third floor were getting restless by the front door. Susan had her hands full trying to keep them quiet. She expected the RD to walk out of her apartment any minute because of all the noise she was trying to suppress. Finally, Mr. Trees gave the all-clear signal, and Carson joined him.

"What happened?" Carson asked.

"The watchman was in the dining hall," Mr. Trees responded. "The girls almost walked right out into the open. Walter would have spotted them for sure."

Carson and Mr. Trees hurried the third group of girls to North Hall. Carson caught himself smiling when it started to look like they might be able to pull off this stunt. Only one more group in Mason remained.

Carson and Mr. Trees were beginning to get nervous because the last group of girls hadn't appeared in the lobby of Mason Hall. They had lost track of the night watchman's whereabouts and were standing out in the open. When Carson spotted Paige bounding down the steps with the rest of the girls, their wait was no longer a concern.

"Is this all the girls who are coming?" Carson asked in a hushed tone.

"You've got them all," Susan whispered. "I can't tell you how much fun this has been. Thank you for including me."

"You're welcome. Are you coming with us? These are your girls," Mr. Trees added.

"I think it would be better if I stayed here. If trouble comes, I can tell the RD that the girls are safe in North Hall," Susan said.

"Good point," Mr. Trees responded. "Carson, we have to get moving."

After Carson and Mr. Trees guided the last group of girls to North Hall, no one was in the lobby to let them in when they arrived. Twenty brightly dressed girls carrying bedding would be easy to spot standing under a bright security light. They needed to get the girls inside quickly.

"Looks like we're going to have to let ourselves in," Carson told Mr. Trees. "I'll see you in a minute."

Carson ran around to the side of the building and squeezed through the first-floor window he had unlocked earlier. He quickly made his way through the dorm and out into the lobby.

"Right this way, girls," Carson said. "The party is downstairs."

Carson stood on the landing of the steps leading to the basement. He estimated they had collected more than eighty girls so far. Mr. Trees continued to guard the front door while the last of the girls moved toward the stairway. Carson breathed a sigh of relief, realizing that his job was probably done for the night unless some unexpected trouble came their way. Their plan was being executed flawlessly.

Paige positioned herself to be the last person in line as the girls descended the stairs. She stopped in front of Carson carrying her blanket and pillow under her left arm. She grabbed his neck with her free hand and pulled him toward her, completely catching him off guard.

"You could have told me what you were planning," she whispered as her lips tickled his ear.

"For all I knew, you could have been a spy for the sophomores," Carson countered, fully aware that she was making him blush.

She pressed her lips against his neck before releasing him. Carson's face reddened. He couldn't very well make a scene in front of all these girls, so he hurried up the stairs to join Mr. Trees.

"I hope this plan works . . . especially for you, Paige," Carson whispered to himself.

"Are you sure you don't want me to go with you?" Carson asked his friend.

"Clara and I should be able to manage ten girls," Mr. Trees countered.

"I wished I would have thought to buy some walkie-talkies. They would really come in handy right about now."

"We're amateurs. We were bound to forget something."

"Get yourself back here in one piece," Carson said.

CHAPTER TWELVE

Carson sat in a darkened corner of the North Commons lobby, keeping an eye out for the night watchman. The smell of Paige's perfume lingered in his nostrils. He couldn't get over the effect that she had on him. She was his equal in so many ways. He loved the way she challenged him with her wit and charm. Maybe it was time for him to tell her how serious his feelings were toward her.

The noise from the large gathering beneath him reached his ears in the lobby. He was happy the freshman girls had a chance to enjoy themselves instead of being subjected to a throng of initiation practices.

I hope the noise doesn't become a problem, Carson thought.

Nearly an hour had passed since Mr. Trees left to get the girls from Omega Hall. Carson was starting to worry. He knew he should have insisted on going with him. This was his plan, and his friend shouldn't have to suffer the consequences if something went wrong.

He finally spotted the silhouette of Mr. Trees scurrying through the courtyard toward North Hall. It was nearly two thirty in the morning, and he was alone. Something bad must have happened.

"Where have you been?" Carson asked.

"I had to take the girls back to the dorm. A group of kids were hiding in the apple grove when we tried to cross Townline Drive. They pelted us with apples."

"I wonder who they were."

"I recognized a couple of them. They were students. Apparently, we aren't the only ones who know initiation is tonight."

Mr. Trees continued. "You should have seen the chaos, Carson. Those poor girls were running all through the neighborhood screaming. They left a trail of blankets and pillows. Clara and I finally got them calmed down, and we started to gather up their stuff when I heard a police siren. At least I got the girls back to the dorm before the police arrived."

"The police? Oh man!"

As they were talking, the lobby doors began shaking violently. Someone was pounding their fists on the glass. Carson and Mr. Trees emerged from the shadows and spotted Lorne, vice president of the sophomore class, standing outside. Lorne had been alerted by the sophomores in Mason that the dorm was virtually empty. The freshman girls were missing. Lorne was clearly agitated. All the plans his team had made for initiating the freshmen were in jeopardy.

"Stay inside and let me handle this. I'm friends with his older brother," Carson said.

"What do you want me to do if fists start flying?" Mr. Trees asked.

"Come out and help me of course," Carson answered, laughing. "Seriously, I'm a lover, not a fighter. I should be able to outrun him easily."

"What if he comes after me?"

"Then, go wake the RD."

Carson and Mr. Trees jumped when they both felt a hand on their shoulder. Mr. and Mrs. Baumgardner were standing behind them. A phone call, not Lorne's pounding on the glass, had woken them up. Mr. Baumgardner went outside and confronted Lorne about his behavior. A heated discussion between the two of them followed. Carson was relieved when he saw Lorne leave. When Mr. Baumgardner returned to the lobby, he wanted answers. Carson decided to let Mr. Trees do all the talking.

"Lorne was looking for a group of girls from Mason. You wouldn't happen to know what he was talking about, would you?"

"That depends," Mr. Trees said diplomatically. "There are some girls having a party down in the basement, but who's to say those are the girls he's looking for?"

By this time most of the girls in the basement had drifted off to sleep. So it would have been quiet enough for Renee to hear the disturbance coming from the lobby. She climbed the stairs to investigate. It just so happened that Renee and Mr. Trees were both RAs who reported to Mr. and Mrs. Baumgardner, so the situation they found themselves in was not as tense as it could have been. The RD shook his head in disbelief when he and his wife peered into the basement and saw all the girls sleeping on the carpet.

"You should know that the dean of students has called for a bed check. The campus is in a full lockdown. You men need to go back to your room. We'll figure out how to handle the situation with the girls," Mr. Baumgardner said.

Carson and Mr. Trees hurried back to their room and got ready for bed.

"What were you doing while I was out risking my neck to bring those girls over from Omega?" Mr. Trees asked.

"I was guarding the lobby like we agreed. Why?"

"It looks to me like you were doing more than that?"

"What are you talking about?"

"Take a look in the mirror, Shy Guy."

Carson smiled when he saw the smudge of red lipstick on his neck. Paige continued to be a handful.

"Whoever she is, I hope she's worth it. You could use a little happiness in your life," Mr. Trees added.

"Her name is Paige. And trust me, she's worth it."

The two friends were in their beds pretending to be asleep when Mr. Baumgardner stopped by about thirty minutes later for the bed check. He flicked the lights on and off quickly; he must have seen them in their beds.

"I don't know how you managed it, but your little stunt was quite impressive. Good night, men," Mr. Baumgardner said as he was leaving.

The next morning Carson and Mr. Trees expected to be called in for questioning by the dean of students. Carson had spent what was left of the evening trying to figure out what he was going to say. He was prepared to take sole responsibility for the prank and shield his friends from any repercussions, but the two of them were never called in. It wasn't until later in the day that they learned theirs wasn't the only disturbance on campus last night. Apparently, Lorne's disorderly conduct across the entirety of the campus searching for the freshman girls had caused more chaos than the apple throwers.

As the day wore on there wasn't a single report of a student getting reprimanded. Perhaps there were just too many students involved. But that didn't mean the administration failed to take swift and decisive action. The unofficial word being passed around campus was that the administration had canceled all initiation proceedings.

Carson, Mr. Trees, Clara, Renee, and Susan couldn't take sole credit for saving the freshman students from initiation, but they had accomplished something no one else had ever done. Unfortunately, they couldn't tell a soul about it.

It had been an exhausting week for Carson. He kept to himself Friday afternoon and tried to focus on his homework. Switching his major to biology had certainly made his course work more interesting than social work, but Carson found the curriculum to be much more challenging. After supper, when the music got too loud in the dorm, he headed for the library.

The campus library was small by university standards, but it managed to accommodate the needs of the students. Carson couldn't find a quiet spot on the main floor. Students were still buzzing about initiation being canceled. So he descended the stairs to the lower level and found an empty table in the back corner of the room.

Half an hour later, he fell asleep with his head pressed against an open textbook resting on the table in front of him. He thought he heard someone clear their throat and snapped to attention.

"Can I sit at your table? I was studying in the dorm, but it got too noisy," Paige said.

"Be my guest."

"Thank you for rescuing us last night. Who knew your idea would actually work! You've become a popular guy overnight. I know a number of girls who will want to go out with you now."

"Did you have someone specifically in mind?"

Paige simply smiled at him.

"I guess not. Did you get in trouble after my roommate and I were told we had to leave?" Carson asked.

"That's the funny thing, they let us sleep there all night," Paige replied.

"I'm glad everything worked out for you," Carson said. "Oh, and I meant to tell you that those cute red sweatpants you were wearing last night have a small rip pretty high up on the back of your leg. It's kind of revealing. I just thought you might want to know."

She reached across the table and slapped his hand. "Carson, have you been looking at my butt?"

"What do you think?"

They both fought back smiles as they turned their attention to their textbooks and began reading.

"Paige," Carson said, "I lied. There's no rip in your sweatpants. I was just trying to get back at you for the lipstick thing."

"Touché," Paige said. "Carson, can I ask you a serious question?"

"Of course," Carson said.

"The other day when we talked under the stars, I saw a side of you I've rarely seen before—the honest Carson. What's with the whole suave thing?"

"I'm assuming you want the truth," Carson answered. "You are a very pretty girl, Paige. When you went to that campus movie with me at the beginning of the semester, you caught me off guard. Your beauty goes way beneath the surface. I wasn't expecting you to be such an incredible person. The suave thing is a cover-up. I didn't want to scare you away by revealing the effect you had on me."

"Wow, more of the honest Carson," Paige replied as the color rushed to her cheeks.

"Since we're baring our souls, is there anything you'd like to share?"

"Um, I'm not sure if I want to admit this, but here goes . . . When we were out under the stars and I told you I had to get back to my room, that was a cover-up. You got me flustered with your truthfulness. I thought I had you figured out, someone I could flirt with but could never trust. But I started having feelings for you I never imagined I could have. I needed to get away from you so I could think."

"I see."

"Oh, no you don't. I just bared my soul and all you have to say is, 'I see'?"

"What do you want me to say? Look, I've been hiding my feelings from you, and you've been hiding yours from me. I think that about sums it up."

"Could I see more of the honest Carson and less of the suave Carson in the future?"

"If you think you can handle it," Carson answered, breaking into a big grin.

For the next two hours they studied. Paige glanced up occasionally at the man sitting across from her. If she had to guess, Carson was doing the same thing, but she couldn't catch him in the act. It was hard to concentrate on her studies because she wanted to know what he was thinking.

Ten minutes before the library closed, Carson and Paige left the library. He said good-bye to her outside the library instead of walking her back to her dorm. He thought he detected a look of disappointment on her face. Carson was trying to be very careful around her. He needed to know how she felt about him before he dared trying to take their relationship any further.

But he couldn't bring himself to talk to her before his big race. If Paige wasn't interested in a serious relationship with him, he'd be devastated. Carson concluded that it would be better to tell her after the race. Then, if the walls were going to cave in on him, he'd just have to deal with it.

Carson stopped in to see Fly when he arrived back at the dorm. As always, he was in a good mood. Fly invited him in to have a chat.

"I had an interesting conversation with Paige tonight in the library," Carson said.

"What was it about?" Fly asked.

"Apparently, she has taken an interest in me. She wants to see more of the honest Carson and less of the suave Carson."

"If you play your cards right, I think she might fall for you, Carson."

"How can I do that when I'm fighting to keep my own head above water?"

"What's that supposed to mean?"

"I'm afraid I've already fallen for her, but I'm trying not to make it obvious. At least not until I think she feels the same way."

"And what would it take for that to happen?"

"I don't know," Carson said. "Maybe if we could get away from this campus and sit down and talk things out."

"I've never seen two people trying so hard *not* to fall for each other. You know it's obvious to her friend Louise and me that you two are a train wreck waiting to happen . . . and by train wreck I mean falling head over heels in love with each other."

"I've made mistakes in the past and broken some girls' hearts. I don't want that to happen to Paige. She's like no other girl I've known. I just can't deal with this right now with the cross-country meet coming up on Wednesday. I need to wait until after the race. You're my number one spy; what do you think I should do?"

"Are you asking me for a favor?"

"What if I was?"

"Carson, let me see what I can do," Fly said, slapping Carson on the back.

"Good night, Fly," Carson said.

Carson had the room to himself. Mr. Trees was out with Clara, no doubt celebrating the fact that they'd had a part in getting initiation canceled. Carson climbed up into his bunk with his Bible. His last home meet was weighing heavy on his mind. After his performance at Houghton, he wondered if a sub-thirty-minute finishing time was still possible. Had muscle fatigue set in? His legs felt like they had recovered from the Houghton meet. It seemed more likely that the battle he faced was in his mind. He needed a reason to believe so that he could accomplish his goal. He thought about his conversation with Coach on the first day of the semester. Turning to Philippians in his Bible, he read, "No, dear brothers, I am still not all I should be, but I am bringing all my energies to bear on this one thing: Forgetting the past and looking forward to what lies ahead, I strain to reach the end of the race and receive the prize for which God is calling us up to heaven, because of what Christ Jesus, did for us" (Philippians 3:13–14). The passage addressed striving for perfection in Christ. But Carson also believed that since the analogy of running a race was being used, he could apply it to his running as well. He needed to forget the results of the Houghton race and hold on to the fact that he ran 30:18 against Buffalo State. All he needed was to be nineteen seconds faster to meet his goal. Carson made up his mind that between now and Wednesday he would focus only on his time from the last home meet. He fell asleep believing that if he gave the upcoming race everything he had, no matter what it cost him, then he would have a successful result.

CHAPTER THIRTEEN

Saturday morning the pay phone rang in North Hall. One of the students walking down the hallway answered it and went to wake up Carson. The student told him his mother was on the phone. His mother assured him that everyone was fine. She called to tell Carson that his high school friend Denny was in town for the weekend and she thought he might want to contact him. Carson jotted down the phone number and thanked his mom. He hung up the phone and went back to bed.

He gave his friend a call after lunch and arranged to pick him up later that evening. Denny's family lived across the street from Carson's house. The two families had known each other for well over a decade. Even though three years separated the two young men, they still were able to form a special friendship. They shared a common taste in music, mainly Olivia Newton John and Electric Light Orchestra. Growing up, they could talk to each other about almost anything, especially girls.

Denny was now nineteen, and Carson was twenty-two. A big man, Denny was two inches taller than Carson and about forty pounds heavier, most of which had turned into muscle. When Carson had last seen him, Denny had thin straight blond hair that almost touched his shoulders. Like Carson, he was caught up in the CB radio craze and went by the handle of Wookie, which he took from the character in the movie *Star Wars.* Recently their paths had diverged: one chose college, the other chose the army.

"What brings you home?" Carson asked.

"I got a weekend pass," Denny answered. "I've just finished basic training, and I'll be heading to Alaska soon."

"That explains the buzz cut. Is basic as hard as they say?"

"We had a couple of wise guys in our platoon, which made things difficult for the rest of us."

"You look good. I wouldn't want to mess with you," Carson said, laughing. "So, what will it be?"

"How about a milkshake from Ho Jo's?"

"You got it!"

Two miles down White Road they came to a familiar bend in the highway.

"I tried to take this corner doing almost fifty a few days ago and spun out. I must be getting rusty," Carson said. "Do you still have your Road Runner?"

"When I joined the military, I figured I didn't need it anymore," Denny answered. "Hey, is Mr. Trees still around?"

"Believe it or not, he is my roommate. We are both set to graduate this year. Give him a shout on the radio. If he's in his car, he'll be on the air."

"Break one-nine. Break one-nine. Mr. Trees, you got your ears on?"

There was no reply. Wookie waited a few minutes and tried again.

"This is Mr. Trees, come on back!"

"Mr. Trees, I hear you five by five. This here's the Wookie, how've you been? We're going out for a milkshake; do you want to come along?"

"It's great to hear your voice friend. You must be with Shy Guy. Tell him to pick me up at Florence Nightingale's place. What's your twenty?" Mr. Trees asked.

"On Main Street, about five minutes away," Denny replied.

"Ten-four, good buddy, over and out," Mr. Trees answered.

"Carson, who's Florence Nightingale?" Denny asked.

"It's his girlfriend, Clara. It wouldn't surprise me if they ended up getting married this summer."

"What about you, Carson, do you have a girlfriend?"

"Let's just say I'm working on one and leave it at that."

It was a special night for Carson to be able to share a milkshake with two of his closest friends, both of whom had played a role in guiding him back to the university. Denny, still in high school back then, helped Carson through countless lonely nights, talking about girls, cars, and their futures. He convinced Carson that he needed a plan for his future, because drifting through life was not a strategy.

Carson would always be indebted to Mr. Trees for his help. At Ho Jo's, Denny talked about the army and about his girlfriend, while Mr. Trees talked about his future in ministry and about Clara. Carson talked about cross-country but didn't feel comfortable taking about Paige because he wasn't sure where their relationship was headed. Carson found this ironic because he was the one they always teased as being a ladies' man, yet he didn't have a girl he could talk about.

On the way back to Denny's house they found themselves on White Road once again. The car in front of them was driving slowly, so Carson pulled out to make a pass. The other car sped up enough to prevent the pass. Carson had to duck back in behind the lead car to let an oncoming car by. When he pulled out a second time to pass, he drove up beside the other car, and they continued down the road, side by side.

"I think those two punks want to race you, Carson," Denny said.

"Don't get me killed before I have a chance to ask Clara to marry me," Mr. Trees pleaded from the backseat.

"Nobody is going to die tonight," Carson replied. "This young man is driving his daddy's car and has no idea who they're up against. I'm going to push them up to that sharp bend in the road. He'll will probably stomp on his brakes before he gets there, and we'll sail on by. But if he doesn't, well, we may be in for an interesting ride."

"Lord, have mercy," Mr. Trees blurted out.

"Mr. Trees, maybe you should say a prayer for us. We don't need any cars coming at us right now," Carson said jokingly. "Wookie, if you see one coming, yell and I'll duck in behind these guys."

Denny rubbed his hands together. "This is going to be great!"

Carson increased his speed gradually to inch ahead of the other car. The bend in the road was approaching rapidly. He waited for the other driver to pull even with the Demon. When the other driver did, Carson realized he'd made a mistake. He should have just completed the pass and controlled his entry into the corner; then everything would have been fine. But Carson wanted to show off for his friends and in doing so was putting them all in danger.

"I probably should have passed the guy. Hang on! We're in for a wild ride!" Carson said.

"Lord, help us," Mr. Trees shouted.

"No traffic yet, Carson," Wookie said, laughing.

"Are you sure you can handle this, Shy Guy?" Mr. Trees added.

"Wookie and I have done stunts like this more times than we'd care to admit. Unfortunately, most of them were close calls," Carson replied. "Maybe you should close your eyes. This will all be over in a minute."

Carson downshifted into third gear, causing the engine to rev loudly as the RPMs skyrocketed and sent the tachometer needle up against the red line. He put the nose of the Demon down on the shoulder as he approached the banked ninety-degree corner. The car beside him had not started braking yet. Carson couldn't go any faster in third gear without damaging the engine, so he reduced his speed and let the other car creep ahead of him into the corner. This turned out to be Carson's second mistake.

Carson was in an impossible spot now, but he wasn't about to let his friends know it. He now had to react to the movement of the other vehicle instead of planning his next move. He was left with only one option: to take the corner safely in second gear.

The other driver started to panic as he entered the corner. He didn't have the experience Carson had. The rear of the other car began fishtailing as the young man sawed the steering wheel back and forth while applying the brakes. If he lost control of his car, he'd crash into the Demon. Carson realized he was out of time.

Carson locked up the brakes and jammed the gearshift into second gear. When he released the clutch, the tachometer flew into the red zone causing the engine to scream. The engine was now rotating faster than it was designed to. Carson manipulated the steering wheel to keep the back end of his car from swinging around. The tires screeched as they dragged themselves across the pavement trying to slow the Demon down. Carson was now driving under the influence of adrenaline. Everything around him was moving in slow motion. He inched the Demon even lower on the shoulder where weeds grew up through the gravel. His left side tires had left the asphalt completely and were now dragging across the gravel on the shoulder of the road.

When the tachometer needle cleared the red zone, Carson felt the car come back under his control. Now more than halfway through the corner, he stomped on the gas, filling the air with smoke, gravel, and dust. Fortunately, the car beside him had managed to come to a complete stop. Carson shifted into third and quickly into fourth. Within seconds they were cruising down the road at over seventy-five miles per hour. He eased off the gas and breathed a sigh of relief.

"Mr. Trees, are you still with us back there?" Carson asked.

"Only you could find a way to get yourself into trouble and a moment later find a way to get yourself out of it," Mr. Trees replied.

"I couldn't have said that any better," Carson answered. "How about you, Wookie, you okay?"

"That was fun. You made me wish I still had my Road Runner."

Carson pulled into Denny's driveway and said good-bye to his friend. Mr. Trees switched to the front seat before they headed back to school.

"Carson, why do you drive the way you do?" Mr. Trees asked.

"I've been asking myself the same question. Someday this car will be the end of me."

The two friends rode the rest of the way back to the university in silence.

When they returned to the dorm, Carson called Paige on the pay phone. He invited her to go to church with him the next day. He and Mr. Trees spent the rest of Saturday evening studying in their room in an effort to unwind after Carson's stunt with the Demon.

Carson walked to Mason Hall Sunday morning and picked up Paige. Together they strolled down through the center of campus to the church. He wanted her to see his more spiritual side because he felt it was important. Most Sundays, church attendance topped one thousand people. Carson and Paige commented on their shared experience on the way to lunch in the dining hall afterward.

"Carson, I really enjoyed church today," Paige said, taking his hand in hers and squeezing it before letting go. "I'd really like to go with you again."

"I was hoping you'd like it. I don't ever want to be afraid to talk about my faith with you," Carson replied.

"I do have one comment, though. My church back home sings their hymns a lot faster," Paige said, laughing.

"Perhaps the people at my church like to chew on their words a little bit."

"So this is *your* church?"

"Yes, I've been coming here since the eighth grade."

Carson wondered how long it would take for someone to start a rumor about Paige and him when they were seen eating lunch together.

❧

Wednesday, the day Carson was waiting for, had finally arrived. It was a gray, windy afternoon. The temperature struggled to reach forty-six degrees. Injuries had taken a toll on the team. The university was down to just six runners.

The university was about to face Oswego, another strong opponent. A respectable crowd gathered for the team's final home meet of the season despite the cold weather. Carson was still in his room when one of the race officials gave both teams a fifteen-minute warning before the start of the race. It was hard to imagine that he would miss the biggest race of his life.

Carson was in his room spending time alone with God. He had read a passage from one of the Psalms, and it had captured his attention. For some reason he felt that he was at the precipice of something that would change the direction of his life forever. The significance of the moment seemed much bigger than the race he was about to run.

He read silently to himself: *Trust in the Lord instead. Be kind and good to others; then you will live safely here in the land and prosper, feeding in safety. Be delighted with the Lord. Then he will give you all your heart's desires. Commit everything you do to the Lord. Trust him to help you do it, and he will* (Psalm 37:3–5).

Lately, Carson found himself trying hard to please God, not because he felt like he had to but because he wanted to. He had been leaning heavily on God, especially over the past few days. His conversation with Paige had lifted him out of a place of despair. But it occurred to him earlier today, while he was walking to class, that he didn't deserve someone like her. He had done things in the past he was not proud of and had hurt people along the way. But God seemed to be reminding him of his undeserved mercy.

God, I am so thankful for the mercy you've shown me. I know you love me even though I don't deserve it. I trust you with my future. Your Word says that You know the desires of my heart. A race may seem like a trifle thing to you, but it is my heart's desire to get a good result today. I'm asking for your help.

Fly walked in the room and saw Carson sitting on the bottom bunk with his face in his hands praying. There was a small puddle on the floor by his feet.

"Carson, you have a race to run. We've got to go. Now!"

"I guess it's a good thing I'm dressed and ready, isn't it?" Carson answered with a calm determination in his voice.

The two of them hurried out of the dorm and down the sidewalk toward the tennis courts.

"Were you crying?" Fly asked.

"Happy tears, Fly. Happy tears."

"Well, you're about to be happier. Paige is down on the course waiting to see you run."

"How did you manage that?"

"Carson, there's more," his friend exclaimed. "She wants to go on another date with you provided you accomplish your goal. You can't hold anything back today!"

"I don't plan on it," Carson replied. "Fly, calm down and save your energy for the race. Before I forget, I want to thank you for looking out for Paige and me. Don't think for a moment that I don't know how hard you've worked at trying to bring us together."

Carson hugged his friend. The two of them arrived at the starting line with only a couple of minutes to spare. He scanned the crowd hoping to spot Paige before the race started. It wasn't until he heard her call his name that he caught a glimpse of her. The two of them exchanged smiles. The sight of Paige cheering for him as he walked to the starting line filled his heart with joy.

CHAPTER FOURTEEN

Paige watched Carson's expression change when the command was given for runners to take their mark. A strong determination registered on his face.

"Spock, can you lead me out one more time?" Carson asked.

"Rookie, I'm here for you. We all know what you're trying to do. You'll probably need a miracle to pull it off, but then again, you've been surprising us all season."

"Thank you, Spock."

"Carson, you can do this," Paige yelled, breaking the silence as the runners waited for the starting pistol to fire.

Carson followed Spock out on the course, running just off his shoulder.

"Stay right where you are, Rookie. Let me block the wind for you a while."

"I'm going to try to stay with you for the first mile if I can."

"I hope you know what you're doing."

The wind chilled his bare legs as he ran past two baseball diamonds and approached the cinder track. He wasn't concerned about his breathing yet. He had too much adrenaline pumping through his system. They exited the track after two laps and headed out into the large open field. Carson managed to keep pace with Spock. When the one-mile marker was in sight, a sudden pain erupted in Carson's right side.

"Spock, I think I'm in trouble! I've got a side stitch," Carson cried out.

"Stay calm, Rookie, it's more common than you think. Make a fist and press hard against it," Spock answered.

"It's bad. I can't breathe. Am I finished?"

"Just keep pressing against it. You'd better slow down. Take shallow breaths and focus on your breathing. You should be okay."

They reached the one-mile mark.

Carson followed Spock's advice. He backed off his pace significantly and began taking short, shallow breaths. He knew he was giving back all the time he gained over the first mile, but there was nothing he could do about it. As he stumbled along nursing his side, two Oswego runners passed him. Carson was still running in fifth position for his team. Tears of defeat formed in Carson's eyes and clouded the course ahead. With five Oswego runners in front of him, their winning season was now in jeopardy.

Coach saw that Carson was in serious trouble and cut across the course to the two-mile mark to find out what the problem was. Carson retreated to the familiar safe place in his mind and began to pray.

God, I need you. I'm in trouble. I don't want to let anyone down today, especially you. Your Word says you give strength to the powerless, and right now that's me. If this pain doesn't go away soon, my race is over. Let me run like I'm capable of. Let me show you what you can accomplish through me.

Carson came to the signpost in the middle of the large field and turned right. He continued to press his fist into his side. The pain felt like it was subsiding. He straightened his posture and followed the wide arc laid out for the runners as they approached the two-mile mark at the base of a hill.

At the two-mile mark Coach yelled, "Carson, are you all right? What's going on?"

"I had a side stitch, but it's almost gone," Carson replied.

"We can win this meet, but we're going to need your help. Are you up for it?"

"I think so."

With the stitch finally gone and his breathing normalized, Carson charged up the hill and ran past the campus buildings on his right. It occurred to him that the side stitch probably cost him any chance of beating his sub-thirty-minute goal, but he couldn't worry about that now. He needed to find someone to run with.

The downward slope of Vine Street was usually where he settled into his normal pace. But he couldn't afford that luxury today. He planned to attack every inch of the course for the remainder of the race no matter what it cost him. Vine Street took him to Townline Drive.

Carson followed the solid white line, which led him back into the large open field. He forced himself to maintain a faster-than-normal pace as he passed the signpost for the second time and headed for Main Street. The design of the course was such that the runners passed close to the crowd when they reached Main. It crossed Carson's mind that if this was a weekend meet, there was a strong possibility that his father would be in the crowd. Sports venues were one of the few places he enjoyed his father's company. Carson heard cheers as he turned onto the road. A woman screamed his name. He wondered if it was Paige. The mere possibility of it brightened his countenance as he battled the onset of pain. Aside from God, she was quickly becoming the most important person in his life.

He was running with reckless abandon now, holding nothing back for the finish.

Coach was waiting for him at the three-mile mark. "Carson, do you think you can run down that Oswego runner ahead of you? He's running by himself, and it looks like he's faltering."

"I'll try, Coach. But I can't promise you anything," Carson said, managing a tired smile.

This section of the course featured a long stretch of roads: Main Street to Vine Street and Vine to Townline Drive. He spotted the Oswego runner ahead of him and locked his focus on the man's legs, something Coach had taught them to do when attempting to catch a runner ahead of them. *His legs are my legs,* Carson said to himself, repeating the phrase over and over in his mind.

He saw the runner stumble as he struggled up the hill on Vine Street, which gave Carson a chance to close the gap between them. He charged up the hill in pursuit, ignoring the pain and shortness of breath that came with it. He was gaining on the runner in front of him, albeit slowly.

Carson turned from Vine onto Townline Drive and hurled himself down the grade. He finally caught the Oswego runner at the bottom of the hill but lacked the energy to pass him. He'd pressed himself to the point of exhaustion. He knew that if he ran closely behind the Oswego runner, he could draft off him and annoy him with his breathing, something Carson hated when other runners did it to him. He decided to stay behind the other runner until the guy tired or made a mistake. Now that he caught him, he was not about to let him go.

Once again Carson retreated into his safe place and talked to God.

God, thank you for helping me come back. My strength is about to fail, but I am reminded that your strength endures forever. I am asking for your strength, God. Please give me your strength!

Carson stumbled as he left the pavement before entering the large open field for the last time. He scolded himself for not paying closer attention to his footing. Carson approached the signpost in the middle of the field for the third and final time. He spotted Coach standing there at the four-mile mark. Carson let the Oswego runner get several strides ahead of him so he could hear what Coach had to say without his competitor listening in.

"Carson, do you have anything left to beat him? Believe it or not, your time splits are incredible. You're running way above your normal pace. Don't quit on us now."

"Coach, the Oswego runner just turned the wrong way at the signpost."

"Carson, now's your chance to lose him. Go!"

Coach ran after the Oswego runner to inform him of his mistake. His integrity was evident when he finally caught up to him and convinced the runner to reverse direction. Carson was pressing his pace as best he could, but he was on the verge of going anaerobic. It was way too early to consider that. The final mile led runners down through the center of campus. He felt a sense of nostalgia as he spotted Sharpes Hall, then his dorm, followed by Paige's dorm, the dining hall, and the library. All of them had been such a big part of his life for the past five years.

As he was reminiscing, he was suddenly aware of the Oswego runner behind him, coughing and breathing heavily in his ear.

That guy must be running on pure adrenaline, Carson thought. *I wonder if he can hold that pace all the way to the finish.*

The runner surged past Carson at the base of the hill beside the library. At that moment Carson spotted Coach waiting for him by the cinder track.

"Carson, you can't let him get away. This is your time now; this is your race. Move!"

"Don't worry, Coach, I've got him right where I want him." Carson coughed as he forced his lungs to surrender the words.

It would take every fiber of his being to catch and pass that runner. He spent the next five seconds psyching himself up for a predetermined moment when he would unleash his fury. That moment came when his foot touched the cinders on the track. Instantly, his body exploded into overdrive, catapulting him into the air.

Carson fought to keep his legs underneath him. The length of his stride doubled as he pressed his oxygen-starved legs as fast as they could carry him. His eyes locked on the runner in front of him. He was fully committed now, pressing himself faster. Carson was moving so fast the other runner appeared to be standing still. The gap closed rapidly; twenty yards . . . ten yards . . . five yards.

Had he waited too long?

The finish line was just a few yards ahead. The pain in Carson's body reached a critical point. He commanded his legs to move faster, yelling at them.

"No! I will not let you quit on me!"

In that moment Carson witnessed something he once thought was impossible become possible, and he believed. It didn't matter that he may have lost his race against time. He knew he could beat the runner ahead of him. A Bible verse he'd been trying to memorize came to mind: "So take a new grip with your tired hands, stand firm on your shaky legs, and mark out a straight, smooth path for your feet" (Hebrews 12:12–13). Today he had found strength from another source. God himself was marking out a path for his feet to follow.

The runner ahead of him eased up ever so slightly two strides from the finish line to glance over his shoulder one last time. Carson was so close to him that he could see defeat register in the man's eyes. He grazed the Oswego runner as he surged past him, beating him by a mere half a second.

"Oh God! Oh God!" Carson cried out, repeating the only words his mouth could form.

He managed two more strides before collapsing on the ground. He had pushed himself beyond the limit that his body could take. Spock and Einstein were standing in front of him, having finished the race seconds before him. They helped him to his feet.

"Carson, you should walk a little bit before you sit down," Einstein said. "What a heck of a way to finish the race! You'll remember this one for the rest of your life."

"I can't stand, let alone walk," Carson gasped.

"Here, we'll help you. Put your arms over our shoulders," Spock said. "I suppose you're going to claim that if you hadn't gotten that side stitch, you would have beaten me today."

"Spock, why do you always have to make me laugh when my sides are hurting?" Carson said, struggling to breathe. "I guess we'll never know, will we?"

"It looks like he'll live," Einstein said.

Carson's teammates walked him away from the crowd and lowered him to the ground.

"Did we win?" Carson asked.

Spock and Einstein looked at each other and shrugged. They gave Carson a puzzled look as if neither of them was allowed to comment further.

"Of course we did!" Fly said, arriving on the scene.

But Fly wasn't alone. He brought Paige with him.

"Carson, what an amazing finish!" Paige said, "I'm so proud of you!"

"Paige, forgive me for not standing. I'm too tired," Carson said, finally able to breathe deeply.

Carson rose to a sitting position, extending his arms out behind him so he could remain upright. Paige lowered herself to the ground and nuzzled up to him.

"How's that?" Paige asked.

"I'm sorry I let you down, Paige," Carson said with tears streaming down his cheeks. "I really wanted to beat my goal today, but I got hurt and didn't get the finish I wanted. I want you to know that I gave it everything I had."

"That's not what Fly told me," Paige answered, wiping the tears from his face with her mitten.

"Guys, I think we should be going," Fly said. "Let's give these two a moment alone."

"What did Fly tell you?" Carson asked.

"He said I owed you a date," Paige replied.

"I wish it were true, Paige, believe me I do. I want to go out with you in the worst way, but a deal is a deal. I trashed my time one mile into the race."

"But your time was 29:47."

"That's not possible," Carson countered. "Help me up so I can walk over to the scorer's table."

Carson struggled to his feet. His legs were so tight he could barely stand. Paige rose to her feet quickly to steady him.

"Carson, Fly told me that he would never lie to me about you. Why would he start now?"

"So you're saying I just ran this race in 29:47," Carson exclaimed. "Holy cow!"

Carson thrust both of his arms in the air. He looked at Paige and remembered the scripture verse he read before the race. A merciful God had given him the desires of his heart. He closed his eyes and offered a prayer of gratitude. Carson grabbed Paige and pulled her into a hug. Despite the pain wracking his body, the joy in his heart bubbled over like a fountain. He had wanted to hug her for so long. Paige seemed as happy as he was when the occasion finally arrived.

"Well, now are you finally ready to go out on that date with me?" Carson whispered in her ear.

"It's about time you asked," Paige replied in a whisper so soft it rocked him to the core.

They broke from their embrace when a group of excited fans and teammates came over to congratulate him. After the crowd dispersed, Carson slowly limped back to his dorm with Paige's help. He felt like a warrior returning from battle. The reward for his victory was simply to be with the girl walking beside him.

"Would it be okay if I sat with you and your friends at dinner tonight?" Carson asked.

"Are you sure you're ready to be the topic of conversation?" Paige replied.

"Hmm, maybe I should bring Fly along for moral support."

"That's probably a good idea."

"Paige, I really thought I'd lost my chance to go out with you."

"You have Fly to thank for that. He stuck his neck out for you when almost everyone else warned me to stay away from you."

"Will you give me a chance to prove them all wrong?" Carson asked.

"Rookie, you may be a fast runner, but don't think for a minute that you're done chasing me."

"Paige, I couldn't outrun my grandmother right now."

Carson gave Paige another hug and fought the urge to make it more endearing. After she left, Carson struggled up the ladder attached to the bunk bed and flopped into his bed. He quickly fell asleep.

When he woke up a half an hour later, his leg muscles were in knots. He spent another half an hour doing his pre-race stretching routine. The stiffness abated barely enough for him to walk, albeit with the stride of an elderly man.

CHAPTER FIFTEEN

$\mathcal{S}$itting with Fly at the same table with Paige and three of her suitemates proved to be quite entertaining. Carson received more attention than he wanted. He got in trouble for politely leaving an empty chair between Paige and himself when he sat down, resulting in endless teasing. A few minutes later, Fly used the opportunity to highlight Carson's running prowess, embarrassing him further. And finally, when Paige returned from getting a drink refill, she chose to sit in the empty chair Carson had left between them. Her friends exhorted her to put the moves on Carson, causing Paige to blush.

That evening Carson was listening to music when Mr. Trees dashed into their room. He was breathing so hard that he couldn't speak. Carson turned down the stereo and waited for him to catch his breath.

"Carson, come with me . . . quickly!"

"What's the matter?" Carson asked.

"I want to pull a prank on one of the guys in my New Testament Greek class."

"Is he one of your ministry friends?"

"Yes. The pour guy has been asking girls out since the beginning of the semester, and up until today everyone has turned him down. He just went out with a girl who said yes."

"And what does this have to do with a prank?"

"He left his car running when he went into Mason. I need you to help me steal his car."

"Wouldn't I be breaking one of the Ten Commandments?"

"We aren't really going to steal it."

"We're either stealing it or not stealing it. It's pretty cut and dry from my point of view. I'm pretty sure the police will see it the same way."

"Stop clowning around and come with me."

Carson followed Mr. Trees over to the drop-off zone in front of Mason Hall where Harry Williams's car was parked. For the first time since he had known Mr. Trees, Carson wasn't able to keep up with him. His legs hurt that bad.

Harry was still inside when they arrived. Carson crawled in the passenger seat and left the driving to Mr. Trees. They took the car over to the parking lot separating Sharpes Hall from the church. The two fugitives walked back to North Hall and spotted Harry walking toward them.

"Here, take these keys and put them on Harry's dresser," Mr. Trees said. "I'll keep him busy."

Harry was so excited about his date that he didn't realize his car was missing.

Harry knocked on their door several hours later, "Can you guys help me figure out where I left my car? I completely forgot where I parked it."

Carson cracked a smile and had to cover his mouth with his hand. "I can't. I have some things I need to take care of."

"I'll help you, Harry. Are you sure you can't remember where you parked it?" Mr. Trees said, trying not to laugh.

About an hour later Mr. Trees returned.

"How did that go?" Carson asked.

"I held out as long as I could, but when my legs started getting tired from walking, we happened upon his car pretty quickly," Mr. Trees said.

"And he still thinks that's where he parked his car."

"I didn't have the heart to tell him otherwise."

"And you call yourself a minister?" Carson said, cracking a big smile.

"Don't worry I'll tell him some day."

The next morning Carson stopped in to see Coach. He was busy preparing for the team's seven-hour trip to Nyack, a town just north of New York City.

"Coach, I need to talk to you for a minute."

"Is everything okay?" Coach asked.

"My legs are so tight I can't run on them," Carson said. "Do you think I should go with the team to Nyack?"

"You still have until tomorrow to get loosened up. Why don't you do your pre-race stretching routine and then slowly jog for fifteen minutes. Stretch again after you finish. Wait about four hours and go through that process again. Later tonight try it one more time and see if you can jog for thirty minutes."

"I'll give it a try," Carson promised. "I really want to go to the meet."

"Come back and see me tomorrow morning, and then we'll decide what to do," Coach said. "Carson, your finish against Oswego is something I don't think I will ever forget."

Carson spent his free time between classes following Coach's prescribed routine. His legs slowly loosened up as the day wore on. After supper, Carson called the pay phone on Paige's floor in Mason Hall. Louise answered it and said she thought Paige was in the library. Carson drove over to the drop-off zone in front of Mason and walked into the library. He spotted her sitting at the same table they'd studied at a few days earlier and sat down beside her.

"Hi, Paige," Carson said. "I'm leaving for Nyack in the morning and was wondering if you'd like to go for a ride with me tonight?"

"Oh, Carson, please, please, please can I go?" Paige said, imitating a dreamy-eyed coed.

"You play that part really well."

Paige punched him in the arm. "That wasn't a nice thing to say."

"One of the things I like about you is your playfulness. Promise me you won't ever change."

"That's better."

Carson carried her books for her as they walked to the Demon. He never got tired of the envious looks on people's faces as they passed by his car. Carson politely held the door for Paige as she got in.

"You're such a gentleman," Paige said. "My mother would be proud of you."

Carson started the engine and sat for a moment. It was time to have a serious discussion about where their relationship was headed.

"Carson, what are you waiting for?" Paige asked. "I hope you weren't waiting for me to sit on the console next to you again."

"Let's talk about that since you brought it up," Carson replied. "You made quite an impression on me that first trip to Ho Jo's. You had me eating out of your hand in a span of about ten minutes."

"Carson, since we're being honest, I learned a lot about you from my conversations with Fly. I decided to play the part of a flirt because I wanted to see how a senior guy would treat a freshman girl. You did your best to make me feel comfortable. I was impressed with how engaging you were."

Carson slipped the car in gear and drove down Townline Drive to Union Street. He babied the Demon, trying to show Paige what a responsible driver he was.

"Carson, why are you driving like my grandmother?"

"Because I'm trying to impress you."

"When am I ever going to meet the old Carson?"

"I don't want to lose my chance at getting to know you by scaring you away. Paige, I like you a lot, and I'd like to spend the rest of my time here at the university getting to know you. So much of my past is not pretty. I'm just trying to protect you from it."

"I think we can agree we've both done things in our past that we're not proud of. Don't be afraid to show me where you've been so I can see how far you've come," Paige urged.

Carson stopped the car in the middle of the road. There were no cars coming in either direction.

"You want to see the old Carson?"

"Yes. How different can he be from the runner who looked defeat in the face and refused to lose just so he could go out on a date with a girl he barely knows?"

"Put your seat belt on."

"Are we going to race?" Paige asked, excitedly clicking on her seat belt.

"We aren't going to race on this street. Too many policemen use this road. However, I think you need to appreciate this car's power before you can appreciate its speed."

Carson removed his foot from the brake and hovered it over the gas pedal.

"Ready?"

Paige nodded.

Carson stomped on the gas pedal as he popped the clutch. The engine roared as the tires made a continuous screeching noise, leaving a matched pair of rubber tracks on the street. The screeching didn't end when he shifted into second gear. Paige was pinned to the back of the seat as the car rocketed forward. Carson shifted into third and finally to fourth. The Demon was moving at seventy-five miles an hour in a matter of seconds before Carson back off the throttle.

"We can't drive over the speed limit on this road," Carson said.

"There, was that so hard? Promise me you won't be afraid to show me the real you, old or new! Let me decide whether I like it or not."

"I promise," Carson said as a smile swept across his face. "Are you hungry?"

"You are such a guy! We're having a serious conversation, and you're worried about your stomach."

"I was thinking of taking you to Ho Jo's for old times' sake."

"Well since you put it that way, you can buy me a milkshake." Paige said unbuckling her seat belt and leaning across the console so that her head found Carson's shoulder.

"I'd put my arm around you but then I wouldn't be able to shift gears."

"You just focus on driving, Rookie. Let me see if I can find our song on the tape player."

"Since when do we have a song? You've only ridden with me one time."

"Here it is, "Superman," you should listen to the words sometime." Paige said giving him a wink.

"I guess I better pay attention to it if it's that important," Carson responded. "While I'm away at Nyack will you think about where you'd like me to take you for our date? I'll do the same thing, and we can compare notes when I get back."

"I'd like that. So, it sounds like you'll be thinking about me on your trip then." Paige said smiling.

"I don't have to go to Nyack to think about you."

"Carson, where are we headed?"

"I thought we were going to Ho Jo's."

"You know what I mean. Us—where are we headed?"

"I will not pressure you into liking me, Paige. The fact is I already like you a lot. I've never felt so alive as when I'm with you."

"I like you too. You and Fly are a lot of fun to be around."

"Ouch, you really know how to hurt a guy's feelings. You just put me in the same category as Fly? I was hoping for a little something more."

"You haven't caught me yet Rookie," Paige said laughing.

"Paige, there is another reason why I wanted you to come out with me tonight. I've decided to sell this car. I'm afraid if I don't part with it soon, I won't live to a ripe old age. God only knows why I'm still alive after some of the close calls I've had in this thing."

"Do you have to sell it? I met you in this car."

"Paige, there are practical reasons for getting rid of it. It's hard to start in the winter and it drives terrible in the snow."

"I guess you should probably sell it then," Paige replied. "How will you take me out on a date without a car?"

"I'm not selling it tomorrow."

❧

Friday morning Carson and five of his teammates stacked their overnight bags in the back of the van. Coach passed out brand new warmups to commemorate their memorable season.

"Coach, thank you for the exercise regimen you prescribed. I think it helped. I should be able to run tomorrow but I won't be breaking any speed records."

"I'm glad you're coming with us," he answered. "All right men let's roll!"

After a seven-hour drive, the team split up and stayed overnight with a couple of different families who were friends or relatives of the university students. With the registrar's help, Coach was able to locate students at the university who lived in the area. Funding for the cross-country team had plummeted because of their lackluster performance in recent years. Coach was doing everything he could to save money. Carson was happy he got to room with Fly. That night Carson was lying in bed staring up at the ceiling.

"Fly, are you still awake?" Carson asked.

"Yeah," Fly answered.

"What can you tell me about Paige? You talk to her more than I do."

"That's not true," Fly answered. "Okay, she did tell me she has an older brother and that she thinks the world of her parents. I think she also told me that she and her mother are close."

"I love my mother, but close is the last word I'd use to describe my relationship with her. She has the tendency to drive me up a wall with all her questions."

"You and Paige will make a great couple once you figure things out."

"Make sure you tell her the same thing, Fly. I've fallen for her. I've never met anyone quite like her."

"Good night, Carson," Fly said, smiling to himself. "Sweet dreams!"

The following morning, the runners ate breakfast with the families that housed them and headed over to Nyack College for the National Association of Intercollegiate Athletics (NAIA) district meet. On the ride over Coach told the team he vowed never to sleep in a stranger's house again the night before a meet. In the future, he'd put everyone up in a hotel. He went on to say that the room he stayed in had no door and a couple of cats bothered him all night. To make matters worse someone in the house was playing loud music until well after midnight. Evidently, Coach had not gotten much sleep.

The NAIA district meet turned out to be more of a road race than a cross-country meet, but Carson lacked the strength and the stamina to face the repeated barrage of hills he encountered from start to finish. The course was five and a third miles long, which explained why everyone's times were slower than expected.

Fly won the meet, which qualified him for the national meet in Wisconsin. The team finished third behind St. John Fisher and a strong King's College team. Carson finished in twenty-seventh place and scored fifth on the team with a time of 33.57. He knew from his performance that muscle fatigue had set in. He was happy that he only had one more race to run.

Coach treated the team to an early lunch at a local diner and announced that he had arranged for them to meet Scott, a university alum who was studying law at Columbia University. Scott promised to take the team to Times Square using the New York City subway system.

At first Carson was nervous about being in the "big city." There were times he felt like an ant crawling on the sidewalk as he walked in the shadows of the skyscrapers. But it wasn't long before he was taking in the sights, sounds, and smells of the Big Apple.

One of the highlights for Carson was watching an emotional Fly jabbering on at each new discovery. Fly got so excited at one point that he had to stop at a phone booth and call his mother just to tell her he had walked through Times Square.

Carson thought about Paige the whole trip home. He wanted so badly to make her an important part of his life. She could ask him for anything and he would do it. When he considered where they would go for their date he thought about taking her to the movies, possibly a double feature, and grabbing something to eat afterward. If Paige wanted to do something completely different, he would give in because he liked her that much.

It was well after two o'clock Sunday morning when the team arrived back at the university. Any conversation he hoped to have with Paige would have to wait until later that day. But Carson was completely unaware of what had transpired while he was away. He had no idea that his relationship with Paige was hanging by a thread. His next conversation with her might be his last.

CHAPTER SIXTEEN

Carson slept in Sunday morning. His legs felt tired and sore when he rose and limped to the bathroom. It probably didn't help being cooped up in a van for seven hours on the ride back to the campus. When he returned to his room, he spotted a note taped to the door. Einstein had taken a message that Paige called and wanted to talk to him. He looked at his watch and saw it was half past noon. Carson hurried to make himself presentable, showering and dressing in his red university-issued sweats. If he was lucky, Paige would still be in the dining hall.

A steady rain was falling when Carson left the dorm, so he decided to drive over and park in front of Mason. He arrived a little after one o'clock and spotted Paige sitting alone. The place was almost deserted. Carson prepared himself for some good news. He thoroughly enjoyed the last talk they had. She looked amazing in a pink sweater she wore over a black floral-print dress.

"Hi Paige!" Carson said, as he sat down beside her.

When she looked up at him, it was obvious she'd been crying. Mascara mingled with tears stained her beautiful face. The smile she offered was forced.

"Hello, Carson," Paige replied softly. "How was your race at Nyack?"

"Paige, what's wrong?" Carson asked. "Why are you crying?"

She didn't answer but sat facing forward as if trying to decide what to say. Reaching into the pocket of her sweater, she pulled out a crumpled note and dropped it on the table in front of him. He unraveled the typed note and read it. He felt the color leave his face, which he assumed Paige noticed. A moment later when the color returned, his face turned a shade of red. His hands trembled as he set the note on the table. He made an effort to steady his hands by slowly flattening out the paper. Then, after carefully examining both sides of it as if looking for a clue, Carson slowly folded the note back into its original shape and placed it on the table in front of her.

"Anonymous?" Carson asked.

Paige nodded. She could no longer control the tears she'd been trying to subdue.

"Is this the same girl you broke up with last year?" Paige asked.

Carson didn't immediately answer because he was praying.

Oh God, I need you now. Paige certainly deserves an explanation if she is ever going to completely trust me. I don't know how to talk to her about this without losing her. Why do these things keep happening to us? Please give me wisdom.

Carson finally answered, "No, it's not the same girl."

"The note mentioned an engagement."

"I've never been engaged to anyone, Paige."

"I can see now why you told me you wanted to protect me from your past."

Carson grabbed a napkin and dabbed at the tears running down her cheeks. They sat in silence while Carson tried to think of something to say. He wondered if silence was his best option. If he said the wrong thing, it could potentially end his relationship with the most beautiful soul he had ever encountered.

"The note said to ask about a ring," Paige said, coldly fighting through her tears.

Carson had never been around Paige when she was upset. He didn't believe it was even in her nature before today. When Paige mentioned the ring, it suddenly dawned on him what was going on, and he had a good idea of who was behind it.

"Paige, this note has nothing to do with you. Can't you see that someone is trying to hurt me?"

"Then why did they send it to me?" Paige yelled. "Answer the question, Carson. I want to know about the ring!"

"You know I won't lie to you. That ring has been sitting in a safety deposit box for almost two years."

"So you did buy one for a girl?"

"Yes, but I can truthfully say that no girl has ever worn it."

"You don't get it, do you? No girl would ever put that ring on her finger if it was purchased for someone else."

"Oh," Carson replied. "Tell me what to say, Paige. I can't stand to see you upset."

"I guess I'm wondering when the next surprise is coming. I don't think I can take another one. What else is lurking in your past?"

"I don't have any more secrets that can hurt you," Carson said. "Look, I told you I've made some mistakes, but they're in the past. I can't go back and change them."

Carson gently grabbed Paige's chin and turned her face toward him. He looked into her eyes, and noticed the light was gone from them.

"Paige, I want you to listen carefully to me," Carson said. "Do you want me to leave and never come back? Just say the word and you can be rid of me forever. I don't want to cause you any more pain."

"I don't know what I want," Paige answered, removing his hand from her chin.

Carson sat for a moment with his hands on the table waiting for Paige to make the next move. He half expected her to tell him to get lost.

Paige suddenly grabbed his arm with both hands and held on to it tightly. "No, I don't want you to go."

"I'm willing to do whatever you want me to do."

"I need some time, Carson."

"Can I walk you back to your dorm?"

Page nodded. Carson helped her on with her coat and put his arm around her waist to steady her. When they arrived at the dorm, Paige stood facing Carson, hugging herself. Someone had stolen the joy from her life, and that made Carson very angry. But it wouldn't do him any good to lose his composure in front of Paige. He brushed the strands of hair away from her wet face one by one and gently kissed her on the forehead.

"I'm going to be praying for you, and I won't stop until I know you are okay," Carson said. "Call me if you need anything, day or night. I'm here for you."

Paige seemed too numb to reply. She turned and walked into the building.

Carson spent the next several hours in his room too distraught to show his face in public. He put on an album by Larry Norman. It was one of the few Christian albums he owned. His favorite song on the album, "I Am a Servant," reached into the deepest recesses of his soul.

Like the lyrics said, he was a servant, waiting for God to speak to him. He was a fallen man, living in an imperfect world. Carson felt helpless, questioning his worthiness, but he pledged his soul to God. In that moment, with his spirit broken and his mind reeling, he prayed for Paige. He asked God to deliver her from the pain he had caused.

He wished Mr. Trees was here to talk to. But as usual he was away preaching at his older brother's church. Carson skipped supper and waited for Fly to return to his room. Eventually, he heard his friend's door open.

"Fly, will you go for a run with me? I could really use some fresh air right about now," Carson asked.

"Sure," Fly replied. "Guess where I've spent the last two hours."

"I don't know . . . but I'm sure you're going to tell me."

"You missed the open house in Mason. Paige's door was shut when I got there, but she opened it when she found out I was visiting. She asked if I'd seen you."

"I don't think she wants to see me right now. There's a good chance she'll never want to see me again because of all the pain I've caused her."

"She showed me the note. That was a pretty cruel thing for someone to do to her."

"The note was never meant to hurt her. It was meant to ruin me. Mission accomplished."

"Give Paige some time, Carson. I think she's just confused right now."

"Come and get me when you're ready to run."

The two friends ran around the perimeter of the campus in the rain. Carson pressed the pace, punishing himself. Physical pain was something he could tolerate. Emotional pain was a different story.

"Slow down, Carson, we still have another meet to run Saturday."

"I'll be so glad when the season is over. I'm emotionally and physically exhausted."

"I'm telling you, Carson, you've made a lasting impression on Paige. She's not going to toss her relationship with you in the garbage."

"You know, I just realized that I don't know a thing about her other than what you've told me. How can I help her if I don't know who she is or what she needs?"

"I think there might have been a bad breakup in her past. But you didn't hear that from me."

Carson stopped running. "I was ready to tell her I've fallen for her today; can you believe that?"

Carson wondered if Fly thought the streaks of water running down his face were tears or raindrops. When they resumed their run, neither of them said anything for a few minutes. Carson was unfazed by the bone-chilling rain falling from heaven.

"So you do have serious feelings for her then?" Fly said.

"Of course I do. She's the most beautiful person I've ever met. I think about her every day."

"So tell her."

"I will, when I think she's ready to hear it."

Carson's clothes were soaked through by the time he finished his run. He took a long hot shower and used the opportunity to catch up on his laundry. He couldn't stop worrying about Paige and struggled to keep her in God's hands.

As the night wore on, Carson grew restless and felt compelled to do something. When he returned to his room carrying a clean stack of folded clothes, a thought occurred to him. Maybe a change of scenery would be good for him right about now. Rearranging his room might just do the trick. The idea of doing something nice for his roommate eased the pain in his heart.

Carson enlisted Fly's help to move the sofa and bunk bed. After several attempts, they eventually found a solution that offered the best use of space. A person no longer had to walk around the sofa to enter the room.

As the night grew long and quiet, loneliness crept back into Carson's heart. He felt so distant from Paige when he climbed into his bunk with his Bible. Tears wet his pillow as he prayed for her well-being. He turned to Psalm 23 and read it out loud. "Because the Lord is my Shepherd, I have everything I need! He lets me rest in the meadow grass and leads me beside the quiet streams. He gives me new strength. He helps me do what honors him the most. Even when walking through the dark valley of death I will not be afraid, for you are close beside me, guarding, guiding all the way. You provide delicious food for me in the presence of my enemies. You have welcomed me as your guest; blessings overflow! Your goodness and unfailing kindness shall be with me all of my life, and afterwards I will live with you forever in your home."

As he continued to pray, somewhere in the middle of his prayer he drifted off to sleep.

About quarter past midnight, Carson heard a loud crash. He threw off his blanket and bolted upright in bed. Mr. Trees had returned from Pennsylvania and was muttering words under his breath that weren't part of Carson's vocabulary. They were Southern words, and he hoped they weren't sinful. Mr. Trees picked himself off the floor and turned on the overhead light.

"Lord, have mercy!" he cried out. "What happened to our room?"

"Do you like it?" Carson asked, rubbing his eyes.

"Yeah, it's nice, but next time warn me ahead of time so I don't injure myself.

"Sorry. I had all this energy and decided to put it to good use."

"Since you're awake, I have a bit of good news to tell you."

"You're leaving college to take over your brother's church!"

"And leave you here without adult supervision? Fat chance, Shy Guy," Mr. Trees said, laughing. "Clara and I are engaged to be married."

Carson hopped down off his bunk and congratulated his roommate.

"You two are meant for each other. She'll do a great job of keeping you out of trouble when I'm not around," Carson said.

"Get dressed, Shy Guy. We're going out carousing," Mr. Trees said. "And bring your car keys. I'm hungry."

"Good, I want to hear all about how hard it was for you to convince Clara to marry you."

The two good friends spent about an hour taking in the cool night air. They located the night watchman and followed him around at a distance for old times' sake. The notion that the fun they'd shared together off and on for the last four years was about to dissolve into history made Carson sad. His roommate was about to embark on a wonderful new future with Clara. Carson's future, however, had never been more uncertain.

While they shared a midnight snack at Ho Jo's, Carson told him about the difficult afternoon he had. Mr. Trees saw how badly his friend was hurting. He was training to be a minister, and true to his calling Mr. Trees placed his hands on Carson's bowed head and prayed over his friend.

When they returned to the dorm, Carson had trouble falling asleep. He was worried about Paige. She'd looked distant and confused when he last saw her. Carson had told her the truth, but she reacted as if she didn't believe him or feared he was still trying to hide something. Why wasn't he able to ease her pain? Not even Fly, whom Paige trusted, could get her to see that the note was meant to hurt Carson and not her. Carson believed the note had poisoned her mind.

CHAPTER SEVENTEEN

Monday morning Carson had a hard time staying awake for his eight o'clock physics class after being out late with Mr. Trees. Not a day went by that he didn't wish he'd taken physics in high school. He felt as if he was always playing catch-up with the rest of the class. He needed to get more sleep and spend more time studying if he was going to pass this course. Carson hoped he'd be able to do both now that cross-country was ending and Mr. Trees was getting dragged into the wedding planning process.

After his ten o'clock biology class, Carson made his way to the mailroom intending to post a notice on the bulletin board. He was following through on his decision to sell his most prized possession—his Dodge Demon. Before he reached the stairs, he spotted Sunny emerging from the building. At first, he considered pretending he didn't see him but then thought the better of it. He had done nothing to warrant avoiding Sunny.

"Carson, can I talk to you for a minute?" Sunny asked.

"What's on your mind, Sunny?" Carson replied.

"I wanted to apologize for the things I told Paige about you. That's not something a friend should do. I'm sorry if what I said damaged your relationship with her."

Carson was surprised to hear these words coming from someone who almost never considered anyone but himself.

"Why the sudden change, Sunny?"

"I have this new girlfriend, Denise, and she makes me want to be a better person."

"Apology accepted. We've all done things we're not proud of."

Carson knew the feeling. Paige had the same effect on him. He reached out and took Sunny's hand and drew him into a manly embrace, surprising Sunny. The two of them had never been never close enough for that kind of affectionate display.

"Congratulations on the girlfriend. It looks like your strategy to join the cross-country team worked," Carson said.

"And here you thought I was full of hot air," Sunny replied, breaking into his trademark smile.

Paige just happened to be walking by to witness their embrace. She wondered if it was a coincidence, but considering how God works in the lives of his children, she knew it wasn't. Carson's demonstration of love and forgiveness, he later learned, would begin the process of draining the poison from her mind. She was one of the few people who knew how frustrated he was with Sunny because it almost cost him a chance to be with her. Yet here Carson was showing her again how it was better to forgive someone rather than hold a grudge. And Carson wasn't being shy about it. How many times did he have to show her that he had separated himself from his past?

It had been a long morning without the prospect of seeing Paige. After lunch Carson was in his room trying to relax before heading off to cross-country practice. He loved getting psyched up for practice by playing one of his favorite albums. Today he chose an album by Supertramp and soaked up the lyrics to the song "Lord Is It Mine." For Carson, the lyrics went deeper than the secular artist intended them to. He felt a spiritual connection to God when he listened.

As the music played, Carson affirmed that he had found a quiet place with God when he felt alone. Lately, he was tired of fighting battles he couldn't win. The anonymous note Paige received had cast his world into darkness. He couldn't make sense of what was happening to his relationship with Paige. It felt like there was evil at work, and he had no recourse but to put his trust in God. Carson called on the Lord to show him what to do.

After a third time through the song, Carson came to the realization that he needed to confront his accuser, not in a hateful, vindictive manner but with God's love. He believed God wanted him to love this "enemy" in the same way that God loved him. The person he was about to deal with had been stewing for two years waiting for a chance to pounce on him. Carson vowed to go see Shelley before the night was through. She was the only person he could think of who would be capable of sending such a note.

Carson approached cross-country practice with a measure of sadness. His journey of doing something he loved with his teammates was about to end. He had become not only a better runner this season but also a better person, thanks to Coach and his teammates. He tried to imagine where he'd be if they'd never become part of his race against time. He caught himself wondering why he'd never gone out for cross-country in high school. That would have to remain one of life's mysteries.

After dinner that evening Carson called Shelley and told her he had something important to talk with her about. He was surprised she agreed to meet him. He prayed that God would prevent him from saying anything that would make the situation worse and committed himself to forgiving her (if she indeed was the culprit) before he left his room. Carson nervously walked across the courtyard to South Hall where Shelley was waiting for him in the lobby.

"Thank you for agreeing to see me, Shelley. It's been a long time," Carson said. "I'm not going to beat around the bush. I'm here to talk about the anonymous note you sent to a friend of mine."

Shelley registered a look of shock, and Carson immediately knew it was her. Guilt was written all over her face. He watched her squirm trying to come up with something to say.

"All right, I'm not afraid to admit it," Shelley said sharply. "Who told you?"

"No one. If you hadn't mentioned the ring, I'd probably still be guessing. I'd like to know why you would want to hurt a person like Paige; she's not even my girlfriend. I thought this was a Christian college and we were all supposed to practice forgiveness."

Shelley did not look happy that Carson had brought God into their conversation. Her face grew red.

"Maybe this was the best way I could think of to get back at you. You ruined my roommate's life by breaking up with her. When I saw you hanging around Paige, I figured maybe it was time to play my cards. But you must really care about her, or you wouldn't be talking to me right now."

"Correct me if I'm wrong, weren't you the one who told me it would never work out between Sarah and me? You said her parents would never allow us to be engaged."

"You're right about that!" Shelley answered with an air of confidence. "So, what are you going to do now, turn me in for typing a note?"

"What is this hatred you have for me? I've done nothing to you," Carson responded. "No, I'm not going to turn you in. In fact, I'm not going to say anything to anyone, not even to Paige."

"And why would you do that?"

"Because I've learned that I need to forgive the people who hurt me. You and I both know I'm not perfect. God knows I've hurt enough people. Some of them have forgiven me, and some of them probably never will."

But Carson wasn't finished. "If hating me or making my life miserable gives you some sense of satisfaction, I can live with that. But make it about me and leave Paige out of it. If you had one ounce of decency left in you, you'd apologize to Paige for the pain you've caused her."

"I don't hate you," Shelley replied. "But I don't know if I can ever forgive what you did to Sarah."

"I can live with that. This might sound strange to you, but I've already forgiven you. I wouldn't let myself talk to you until I had. What that means is I won't retaliate or do you any harm. No, I'm praying that you will find peace, and I wish you nothing but happiness, Shelley," Carson said, and he turned and walked away.

Carson didn't know if he'd accomplished anything by going to see Shelley, but his heart was clear. He hoped that Paige could get past the hurt the note had caused her. It didn't make sense to him that she was the one being hurt by his past mistakes.

Carson didn't see Paige for the rest of the week. He practiced with the team and tried to get his homework caught up from his time away in Nyack. He looked forward to his occasional evening runs with Fly because it was the only way he could get news about Paige.

On Friday Coach decided not to hold practice due to the wet and slippery conditions. He told the team to rest because it had been a long season. The van was leaving for the State University of New York (SUNY) Binghamton at seven in the morning. They were going to compete in the New York State Collegiate Track and Field Association meet, their final race of the season.

Carson decided to make good use of his free time and made a trip to the bank. After visiting the bank, he vowed to finish what he started.

Twenty minutes later he arrived at the jeweler where he'd purchased the engagement ring almost two years ago. As he waited in front of a glass case, he pulled the ring out of his pocket and studied it. It's hard to believe that he almost allowed himself to become engaged to a girl he thought he was in love with. But it wasn't love, it was infatuation. He couldn't see it back then, but with time came understanding. He produced the sales receipt from his wallet and handed it to the jeweler with the ring. When they came to an agreement on the price, Carson pocketed the money and felt a sense of closure.

Carson begged Fly to go out for a run with him when he returned to the campus. He hungered for more news about Paige. As they slogged along the muddy sidewalks, Carson told him that he sold the engagement ring that had caused everyone so much trouble. He made it clear that it wasn't a secret, hoping Fly might pass the information along to Paige.

On the morning of November third, Coach drove the team three hours to Binghamton. As the team was warming up before the meet, Coach did something he had not done all season. He asked Carson to address the team. After recovering from the initial shock, Carson collected his thoughts and gathered with the team in a huddle.

Carson began, "This is our last meet. For some of us it's the last collegiate race of our lives. I'd like to take a moment and thank all of you. None of us could have accomplished what we've been able to do this year by ourselves. We're six and four; it's the first winning season for our university in nine years. I've been blessed to have been part of this special team.

"So, let's go out and run the best race we can for Coach. I promise not to make a scene at the finish line like I did against Oswego," Carson said, smiling.

That line drew laughter from his teammates.

"We're going to say 'For Coach' on three. Einstein, would you do the honors?"

Einstein stepped forward and stretched out his hand in the center of the huddle.

"One. Two. Three," he said.

"For Coach!" the team shouted in response.

The team intended to give Coach a gift, his first state meet of his young coaching career. But in many ways, it was the least memorable race of the season. The stakes were as high as they'd ever been. It was a state meet after all, but it had been a long season—too long. Everyone on the team was running on tired legs at this point. In the end, the team was swallowed up by the sheer number of great teams competing in the event. The course itself proved to be more difficult than Houghton due to the severity of some of the hills.

As a team, they finished seventeenth out of twenty-one schools that participated. Carson finished in 120th place, scoring fifth for the team with a time of 31:37. Even Fly had a difficult race, finishing twenty-sixth with a time of 27:18.

Coach called the team together afterward and thanked them for an amazing year. He took the time to share a favorite moment with each of the runners and verbally thanked them for their contribution to the team. He mentioned that he would be flying with Fly to Wisconsin in a couple of weeks for the NAIA national championship meet. The team encircled Fly and "assaulted" him with pats on the back and head from every angle, causing him to writhe like an eel taken from the water.

The ride back to the university would be remembered as one of the quietest trips the team had taken. Everyone was exhausted. Carson's mind was flooded with questions. He was thankful for how the Lord had prepared a path for him to follow this season and yet was saddened by the fact that he could no longer participate in a sport he had grown to love. He was also confused by how difficult it had been to pursue a relationship with Paige. Each time progress was made, it was somehow overshadowed by another setback. Carson found himself praying for a breakthrough in his relationship with her.

CHAPTER EIGHTEEN

Sunday morning Carson went to church by himself and had a wonderful time worshiping the God he served. The pastor's message on the power of forgiveness affirmed what he had experienced with Sunny and Shelley. He'd found peace with God in the middle of the storm he was weathering. Carson hurriedly ate lunch alone in the dining hall, refusing to search for Paige in the crowd. Seeing her without being able to talk to her would only intensify the ache in his heart.

Late Sunday afternoon Carson was relaxing in his room replaying some of the most exciting moments of his cross-country season in his mind. His favorite memory was chasing down the Oswego runner and beating him by half a second. The experience was made sweeter knowing Paige had shared the moment with him.

Carson had lost track of time when the dorm pay phone started ringing. He glanced at his watch and realized he'd probably missed dinner. When it became obvious that no one was going to answer it, he hurried to the phone.

"Hello, North Hall, second floor," Carson said.

"I'd like to speak to Carson, please."

"Paige, is that you?"

"Carson, can you come to Mason Hall. I need to talk to you."

"I'll be there in ten minutes."

Carson could tell Paige was crying but she didn't seem upset with him. He hoped she was okay. He quickly changed into jeans and the T-shirt he received as a souvenir from the state meet. Scrambling about the room, he grabbed his car keys and coat and headed over to Mason Hall. Paige was waiting in the lobby when he pulled into the drop-off zone. Carson trotted into the lobby and escorted her back to his car.

"Do you want to go for a drive?" Carson asked.

"Yes, let's get away from this place," Paige answered.

Paige was flustered trying to get the tape deck in Carson's car to play.

"What's wrong with this thing?" Paige said. "Argh!"

"Easy, Paige. You have to turn it on first," Carson said, smiling.

She fiddled with the tape player, fast-forwarding it to the end and flipping it over before reinserting it into the tape deck.

"There, I found our song!" she said triumphantly.

She sang along with Barbara Streisand. Carson was surprised that she knew all the words. She'd obviously been listening to it a lot. Carson sighed; joy had found its way back into Paige's life. She looked directly into his eyes when she sang, "There's nothing I can't do 'cause I'm with you, I'm superman."

Carson turned down the music as the song finished.

"It sounded like you were crying when I talked to you on the phone," Carson said.

"Carson, I've been so wrong to have doubted you. I'm sick and tired of worrying about whoever this old Carson person is. Remind me never to bring him up again," Paige said, reaching across the console to hug his neck.

"Don't get me wrong, I'm happy for you—us, but why the sudden change?" Carson asked.

"A beautiful woman came up to me at lunch today and started talking to me. I've never seen her before. She asked if I was Paige Stuart and if I knew a guy named Carson. When she mentioned your name, I started getting nervous, you know, wondering if this was another one of your past mistakes I was going to have to deal with.

"But she was very kind and started by apologizing for any hurt that terrible note caused. She admitted that the note was sent to try to hurt you, not me. Then she said that she had misjudged you because you're truly not the same person you once were. A calmness came over my mind, and it set my heart free.

"Anyway, the woman said she knew what it felt like to live with pain. She hoped I could find happiness with you, Carson. I've been crying happy tears all afternoon."

"Her name didn't happen to be Shelley, did it?" Carson asked.

"No, it wasn't Shelley," Paige answered. "She said her name was Sarah."

Carson was speechless. Sarah, the girl he was almost engaged to, had driven back to the university not just to apologize to Paige but to wish her happiness with him. Tears streamed down his cheeks. He was completely humbled by the power of her forgiveness. He bowed his head and gave God the praise that was due him. Carson was learning that when God answers prayer, it's sometimes not just a simple answer but layers upon layers of answers, like ripples spreading out on the surface of the water. He wiped away the tears on his cheeks using the sleeve of his jacket and started the car.

"Carson, are you all right?" Paige asked. "This is good news, isn't it?"

"Let's just say that God is always working on our behalf even when we can't see it, and leave it at that," Carson answered.

"Will you ever be able to forgive me for the way I've acted this week?"

"Believe me when I tell you there's nothing to forgive. I'm just so happy that you found your smile," Carson replied. "But I do have another confession to make."

"Carson, don't you dare drag me through another mess."

"I'm hungry, Paige. I missed supper. Will you go to Ho Jo's with me?"

Paige punched him in the arm and said, "Yes, of course I will."

They drove in silence to Ho Jo's. Paige hugged Carson's arm and wouldn't let go of it. Both of them reflected on the week that almost ended their relationship.

"Paige, where are we headed?"

"Why are you messing with me tonight? You just said we were going to Ho Jo's!"

"Us, I mean—where are we headed?"

"Touché," Paige answered. "Carson, I want to go with you wherever you're going from now on. Whether you know it or not, you've finally caught me."

By the time they reached Ho Jo's, pure joy radiated from Carson's heart. This seemed to him like a new beginning, like God had given them a fresh start.

"Well, it sounds like our date is back on the table then," Carson said as he escorted Paige inside.

While they waited for the waitress to bring them their food, they held hands as they sat across from each other in Carson's favorite booth. The smiles on their faces radiated the unspoken love that occupied their hearts.

"Paige, do you mind if I pray before our food arrives?

"I'd like that," she said.

"God, you're such a wonderful Father. Thank you for bringing Paige and me through a very difficult situation. We are certainly aware of your goodness and ask that you help us to be supportive of one another. Help us to guard our faith in you and in each other. Protect us from the schemes of the enemy of our souls. Thank you for the food that is being prepared for us. In Jesus' name we pray. Amen."

"Amen," Paige added. "Now let's talk about this date that you keep bringing up."

"We don't have to go if you've changed your mind."

"Of course I want to go! A deal's a deal, remember?"

The two of them compared schedules between bites of food. There were only a few weekends left in the semester and none of them would work. The only available day they could come up with was the last day of the semester after they finished their exams.

"Paige, there's one more thing we should talk about," Carson said. "I'm finally selling my Demon. One of the guys on campus is interested. Hopefully we can agree on a price."

"Like that old Bob Dylan song says, 'The times they are a-changing,'" Paige replied. "Maybe it's our time now."

Carson and Paige had a wonderful week together after that memorable Sunday. They ate meals together in the dining hall with Paige's suitemates and Fly. Some days they took walks together in the afternoon. Carson was not shy about holding her hand. When evening came, they studied at their favorite table in the library and hugged each other whenever they parted. Paige seemed eager to attend church with Carson when Sunday came.

Carson invited Paige to the open house scheduled for North Hall on Sunday afternoon. It was a mere formality because Paige was already planning on coming. She learned from Fly that Carson liked carrot cake, so she had one of her friends purchase a slice from a local deli.

Carson was in his room sitting at his desk when Paige arrived. His eyes lit up when he saw the gift. Paige insisted that the only way he was going to get any of it was if she fed it to him.

"You have to learn to trust me," she said, "just like I had to learn to trust you."

Paige sat on his lap and fed him the cake with a plastic spoon. She had fun missing the mark on more than one occasion. By the time they were finished, Carson needed a towel to clean his face.

While Carson was busy cleaning up after the mess they made, Paige examined Carson's record collection. He showed her how to work his turntable and power up the receiver so she could play any record she wanted. She seemed particularly fond of his old collection of forty-fives that he'd acquired back in high school. She played a few of them. At the bottom of the stack was a 1960s tune with a title that made her laugh, "Which Way You Goin' Billy?" by the Poppy Family.

"Seriously?" Paige said, holding up the record.

"Hey, I was thirteen when the girls at camp sang that song to me. I would get so embarrassed," Carson responded, laughing.

Carson immediately realized that he had made a huge mistake. Paige put the record on and listened to it twice, laughing the whole time. By the third time she played it, she knew enough of the words to serenade Carson by singing along using her best dreamy-eyed coed impersonation, which made him blush. He had never seen Paige so happy.

Carson pulled Paige away from the stereo and selected an album by Olivia Newton John. Paige rolled her eyes.

"Hey, Olivia and I have a connection."

"Oh really?" Paige replied.

"Come sit with me on the sofa so we can talk."

"Should I be worried?"

"Of course not," Carson responded.

After they got comfortable, Carson asked, "How am I doing?"

"It sounds like you are asking me to grade you. Let me see . . . This could be fun."

"I guess I'm ready for a little truth telling. Give it your best shot."

"Well, for being an all-around good person I'd give you an A-minus. Only because I haven't seen you help any old ladies across the street yet. For living out your faith, that one's easy, A-plus. The way you handled the situation with Sunny warmed my heart. And I found out this week from a girl named Shelley that you confronted her about the note."

"You weren't supposed to find out about either one of those."

"But I did. Your faith is the main reason I'm sitting here beside you. That, and the fact that you are very cute in those red warm-ups you wear."

Carson started tickling her.

"Hey, I'm not finished grading you yet. Stop distracting me. Let's see . . . yes and of course there's the mom factor. I think my mother would give you a B-minus."

"Wait . . . you told your mother about me?"

"Of course I did. We talk about everything. Are you ready for the last one? I hope you have thick skin. Drumroll, please . . . Are you romantic? I give you a C-plus. The plus was for the anonymous birthday card, a nice touch. Here's a hint that will get you extra credit . . . I like flowers."

"Wow, that's humbling. I guess I have some work to do," Carson responded. "Seriously, Paige, I've been holding back my affection from you. Let me tell you that it hasn't been easy. I haven't taken a vow or anything like that. I just want to get to know you first before I took it to the next level. I made a mistake a couple of years ago mistaking infatuation for love, and it caused someone a lot of pain. I don't want to make the same mistake again."

"Trust me, Carson, I've been there too."

"Are you finished grading me? Because I have an idea I want to run by you," Carson said. "What do you think of me hosting a Bible study next semester down in the basement of North Hall?"

"I'd want to come. That's what I think," Paige answered.

"God has been so good to me, so I wanted to give something back. Nothing fancy. Maybe we could sing a few worship songs, read the Bible, and pray for whoever needs it."

"It sounds like you've been thinking about this for a while."

"I have. I was planning on doing it whether I got a chance to go out with you or not."

"Like I said, faith, A-plus."

It was raining Monday afternoon, so Carson canceled their plans for a walk. Paige was disappointed, but Carson assured her that he'd meet up with her for dinner in the dining hall. He told her he had something he needed to take care of with his roommate. He couldn't very well tell her he was going shopping for flowers.

CHAPTER NINETEEN

"Hey, Shy Guy, climb in that shopping cart and let me push you around in it," Mr. Trees offered.

"Are you serious? You want me to put my life in your hands?" Carson replied.

"You're supposed to be watching out for me, remember. Clara wants you to protect me. So that means you're the one who has to get in the shopping cart."

"I don't think that argument would stand up in court," Carson said, giving in to his friends wishes. "Hold the thing still so I don't break my neck getting into it. Remember, you're going to have to tell my mother and Paige if I get hurt."

"So you do have a girlfriend now. How nice. It must not be serious yet if you put your mother at the top of the list."

Mr. Trees started pushing. Carson was glad the parking lot was almost empty because Mr. Trees was swerving the cart all over the place. The rain earlier in the afternoon had stopped, but the temperature was dropping fast, plummeting to almost thirty-two degrees. A cold wind caused some of the shallow puddles in the parking lot to become slick.

Mr. Trees slipped on a patch of black ice and went down face-first, landing on his stomach. That left Carson freewheeling across the parking lot, trying his best to lean in one direction or another to avoid the remaining light poles. He couldn't stop his journey toward a grass-covered ditch, however. When the front wheels reached the soft earth, the cart pitched forward. Carson was tossed into the ditch where he lay motionless.

"Oh Lordy," Mr. Trees exclaimed, running toward his friend. "Carson, are you all right?"

Carson didn't answer. As Mr. Trees was bending over his friend checking to see if he was still alive, Carson bolted upright, sending Mr. Trees reeling backward. Neither of them could stop laughing.

"Don't ever ask me to do that again," Carson yelled.

"You about gave me a heart attack," Mr. Trees replied.

"I guess that makes us even then. Look, I need to get some flowers for Paige. Why don't you pick some up for Clara. Just because you're engaged doesn't mean you can coast along until the wedding."

Carson sat at their usual table in the dining hall at dinner. He arrived early so he could see Paige's reaction when she saw the flowers. He spotted her in the serving line and pretended not to notice her. It amazed him how he longed to be with her. It had been a long time since he had felt that way about anyone. When Paige finally spotted him sitting with a bouquet of flowers stuffed in a plastic glass beside him, she was overcome with excitement and left her place in line. She ran to Carson and hugged his neck.

"Carson, are those for me? Daisies are my favorite," Paige said. "How did you know?"

"I can't divulge my source, but Fly told me she has been in my camp since the day we first met."

"That's Louise!" Paige said with a confident look on her face.

Carson took Paige's hands in his and looked into her eyes.

"I'm going to miss you over Thanksgiving break," he said.

"I'm going to miss you too. I'll be thinking about you the whole time," she replied.

Carson and Paige survived Thanksgiving without each other. But the holiday did serve to stoke the embers of their feelings for one another. There was no denying that they were in love, even though neither of them would verbally acknowledge it.

Coach put invitations in the mail over the Thanksgiving break inviting all fourteen runners who started the season, and a guest for each, to the fall cross-country banquet to be held Friday on the last day of November. Fly, Carson, Spock, and Einstein hastily prepared a color slide presentation using images donated by Carson's father. They synchronized the slides to the music of Supertramp.

Carson was surprised to learn that his father had taken the slides. He hadn't wanted him to attend any of his meets. College was his world where he lived his life, and home was his father's domain. Even though it felt awkward, Carson thanked him for the images.

Carson and Fly arranged another "nondate" with Paige and her close friend Louise. Louise was an attractive girl about the same height as Fly. She had brown eyes and styled her brown hair in a wedge, the style made popular by the Olympic figure skater Dorothy Hamill. Louise was one of the few voices that Paige listened to concerning her relationship with Carson.

Word got out that members of the cross-country team were going to wear sweaters, ties, and dress slacks to make it a more formal affair. The hope was that this would encourage the ladies attending to wear dresses. When Carson picked up Paige in Mason, he was stunned when he saw her in a red dress.

"Paige, you look absolutely beautiful!" Carson exclaimed. "I don't think I'll be able to take my eyes off of you tonight."

Paige laughed, "It's only a banquet. Wait until you see me when I really dress up."

"You look pretty, Louise," Fly said. "For a nondate, that is."

"Thank you. I'll be sure to be on my best behavior tonight, so you won't have anything to apologize for," Louise said with a wink.

"We'd better get going," Carson said.

They enjoyed a good meal and a brief but meaningful program put together by Coach at the Copper Kettle. The slide show went off without a hitch thanks to Einstein's patience and wizardry. Coach handed out trophies to two of the team's outstanding runners. Fly was awarded the most valuable runner award to cheers and a standing ovation. Coach highlighted Fly's 127th place finish at the national meet in Kenosha, Wisconsin. Einstein was given a senior award for his leadership and consistency at finishing in one of the top four places each race. Carson was happy for his teammates.

The night took an unexpected turn for Carson when Coach announced that there was one more award he wanted to hand out.

"Normally, a coach would have to pour over the stat sheets of several players and wrestle with which one to give the most improved runner award to. This year that wasn't the case. There is only one runner on this team who deserves this honor," Coach said. "Carson, would you come up here please and receive this award. You are one of the reasons this team was able to finish the season with a winning record."

Carson was humbled by the recognition as he rose to his feet. Paige offered him a congratulatory hug. To his surprise his teammates rose to their feet and applauded. Carson thought back to earlier in the season when he wondered, in his competitive nature, what could be gained by finishing near the back of the pack, if anything. He concluded that some events in life, though they seem insignificant, can become the foundation for great achievements. Caron realized that God had placed him in the right place at precisely the right time.

"I couldn't accept an award like this without my teammates standing here beside me. Without them I couldn't have accomplished anything. Would you guys come up here and join me?" Carson asked.

The runners scrambled from their seats to join him at the front of the room. The rest of the guests applauded. Carson looked out at Paige and saw her dabbing happy tears from her cheeks. Louise offered Paige a supportive hug. Carson was too far away to tell what Louise was saying to Paige, but whatever it was made them both smile. Carson took a moment to hug each member of the team and say thank you. There was truly something special about this team.

Once the team members had returned to their seats, Coach called eight of them forward. At Coach's discretion, athletic letters were distributed to runners who had made a significant impact on the team's performance. He rewarded any runner who had factored directly into the scoring. Carson held his letter next to his heart and looked heavenward, thanking God for giving him yet another of his heart's desires.

Afterward, Fly, Carson, Louise, and Paige returned to the dorm and changed into street clothes. Everyone agreed a trip to Ho Jo's was in order so the celebration could continue. The night ultimately ended with a bubble gum blowing contest, which Louise won. It was truly a night to remember.

When the appointed Friday came in mid-December, Carson got up early and picked up the local newspaper at the supermarket in town. He joined Fly for a late breakfast in the dining hall. The place was nearly deserted because many of the students had already left the campus for the holiday break. Carson had finished his final exams the day before, but Paige was in the middle of taking her last test.

"What's with the Superman T-shirt?" Fly asked.

"It's kind of a surprise for Paige," Carson replied. "She's into Barbara Streisand's *Superman* album."

"You've really fallen for this girl, Carson. I knew you would."

"It's hard to believe the semester is over. I can't believe everything that's happened in such a short span of time," Carson said.

"I think a big thank-you is in order, Carson. I was so homesick when I got here. You've been such a great friend to me from start to finish," Fly replied. "Those evening runs we had together meant more to me than you could possibly know."

"Paige and I have certainly kept you busy trying to bring us together. If elementary education doesn't work out, you should explore becoming a dating coach."

"I've never seen two people so meant for each other."

"Well, I should be thanking you for all the drama you put up with. When I'm old and gray, it's friends like you I'll miss the most."

"What's the newspaper for?"

"I'm trying to find the perfect movie to take Paige to tonight. We're finally going out on that date you arranged for us."

"I'm leaving this afternoon for Maryland, so I won't be around to clean up the mess if things fall apart," Fly said, laughing as he stood up to leave.

"Take care, my friend, and Merry Christmas!"

Carson spread the newspaper out on the table and sipped his coffee. He found a movie theater that was playing a double feature. He was excited to see that both movies looked like romantic comedies. It's hard to imagine that after all they've been through together, they were calling this their first date.

The snow fell softly outside, coating the ground with a blanket of white. There's only one thing he wanted this year for Christmas, a chance to sweep Paige off her feet. Carson bowed his head and said a prayer for her as she took her last test.

Carson went back to his room and started packing for the three-week Christmas break. He wasn't looking forward to going home. In fact, he dreaded it, mostly because his relationship with his father had soured over the past three years. The two of them didn't see eye to eye on many things, like the music he listened to, the girls he dated, and the purchases he made, such as his motorcycle, his stereo system, and the Demon. It would be one thing if Carson was relying on his parents for the money to pay for college. But he was paying his own way. In Carson's mind, the less he saw of his father over the holidays, the better.

Carson shook off the thought. He refused to let anything spoil the night he had planned with Paige. He searched his heart to find peace, listening to a new album by Love Song that he'd acquired. The song "Little Pilgrim" was quickly becoming a favorite. Like the song said, he was walking down the road of life and had found what he was looking for in Jesus. Fly stopped in to see him before he left. It was the first time Carson had seen his friend tear up. They had fought together on the cross-country battlefield and had emerged victorious.

Carson didn't try to contact Paige after her exam. He figured she needed time to say good-bye to her suitemates. At six he put on his best pair of jeans and slipped into his wooden clogs. He reached into his closet and grabbed his latest purchase, a fleece-lined suede vest with a hood. After rummaging through his top dresser drawer, he was able to find his high school class ring and put it on his finger. He hoped to give it to Paige someday.

Paige looked amazing in her pink sweater and jeans. She wore a blue ski jacket to ward off the cold. Her green eyes danced with excitement as Carson opened the car door for her. Maybe she'd wanted this night to come as badly as he did.

"You look handsome," Paige said as Carson got in the car. "Will you be warm enough in that vest? Wait, what? Is that a Superman T-shirt?"

"Why, yes it is," Carson said, smiling. "Remember, I'm a runner. We don't need much to keep us warm."

"So what movie are we going to see?"

Carson held up two fingers as he started up the Demon and left the school grounds. Paige started up the tape player and fell back into the bucket seat. She sighed, relaxing for the first time all day. For her, it was a perfect moment in time.

"A double feature?" Paige said. "Do you intend to keep me out late, Rookie?"

"I have the feeling that this is going to be one of those nights that I won't ever want to end," Carson replied. "Anyway, we are going to see *Foul Play* and *Heaven Can Wait*."

"I'm looking forward to having so much fun with you tonight, Carson. I could barely concentrate on my last test today."

They arrived at the movie theater, bought a bucket of popcorn, and agreed to share a large container of soda. They picked seats in the center of the theater and waited for the first movie to begin. They chatted about Christmas traditions and their families. Paige was surprised to learn that Carson was one of five siblings. Carson noticed several similarities in how they celebrated Christmas.

Foul Play turned out to be a murder mystery. But no one could deny the chemistry between Goldie Hawn and Chevy Chase. He proved to be her knight in shining armor. As the final credits rolled, "Ready to Take a Chance Again," a Barry Manilow song, played. Paige grabbed Carson's hand and held it as the song played. She rested her head on Carson's shoulder as she listened carefully to the lyrics. During the intermission, they laughed and talked about the "foul play" they had endured just to be sitting together in the theater.

Heaven Can Wait was a sports movie about a football player. Carson was glad that Paige enjoyed the movie as much as he did. In the movie, Warren Beatty and Julie Christie were drawn together by an unlikely set of circumstances. Carson couldn't help but draw parallels to his relationship with Paige. In the end it was the love the two actors saw in each other's eyes that kept them together against all odds.

Carson took Paige to McDonald's after the movie. A good portion of that time he spent trying to memorize her face while they talked and fed each other French fries. He wanted to remember exactly how she looked when they were apart. He loved her kind eyes, her warm smile, and the way her curly hair fell on her shoulders. Carson didn't know it then, but Paige was studying him for the same reason.

"I'm transferring the title to the Demon to the new owner tomorrow. He's taking it home to Pennsylvania," Carson said as they were driving back to the dorm.

"Carson, this car was so much a part of who you were," Paige said. "I'll do my best to help you try to forget it."

"I'm going to hold you to it," Carson replied as they pulled into the drop-off zone at Mason Hall. "Paige, I'll remember this evening for a long time."

As they stood facing each other in the lobby, Carson let his hands rest on Paige's waist. It felt so natural being with her, like she was meant to be part of his life. They looked into each other's eyes. There was nothing awkward about the moment as the seconds passed.

"Fly told me you sold the engagement ring, and now you've sold your car," Paige said, raising her lower lip as if she were pouting. "What do you have left to hold on to?"

"It's called letting go of my past," Carson replied, smiling, touching her pouting lips with his finger. "I rather hoped I'd have you to hold on to."

"I led you right into that one, didn't I?"

"Yes you did."

"You gave me the answer I was hoping for," Paige responded as her expression turned serious. "I've fallen for you, Rookie. I don't want you to hold anything back from me anymore."

Carson pulled Paige close and kissed her gently, sliding his lips across hers. He felt the tension in her body melt and wondered if she was experiencing the same fireworks in her head. Carson later learned that she had never been kissed like that before.

"I've fallen for you too," Carson said. "Would it sound corny if I told you I've dreamed about this moment, about being here with you and holding you in my arms?"

"No, because I've had the same dream."

The couple held each other for a long moment.

"If I don't see you before you leave, Merry Christmas, Paige. I hope you get exactly what you ask for this Christmas."

"Oh, Carson, I already have!" Paige said as she threw her arms around his neck.

Carson kissed Paige again before letting her go, then watched her ascend the stairs one last time.

Paige and he had crossed a threshold so many people around them had tried to prevent. In his mind 1980 brimmed with possibilities, and he was eager to see where the new year would take them.

If you would like to email the author to comment on this novel or express your support for a sequel, email him at wmroushey@gmail.com

ACKNOWLEDGMENTS

$\mathcal{I}$ would like to thank Jesus Christ, my Lord and Savior, for gifting me with the ability to capture words on a page and the insight to form sentences that can be used for his glory.

My thanks go out to the following people:

My loving wife and college sweetheart, Patty, for her unending love and support. She is my inspiration for *The Race Against Time*.

My writing coach, Yvonne Kanu at WordPolish Editorial Services, for seeing the potential in my manuscripts and encouraging me to take risks in my writing that I normally wouldn't take.

My editor, Deb Hall at The Write Insight, for patiently and methodically correcting all my grammar, punctuation, and point of view challenges. You have truly made my manuscript sparkle.

The team at Illumify Media Global, for designing the best book covers and for doing an amazing and professional job publishing and marketing my book.

My alma mater, Roberts Wesleyan University, for equipping me with head knowledge and heart knowledge. For patiently providing an environment where I could blossom into a man of God.

My cross-country coach, Craig Hayward, for his insights into coaching and his incredible memory of the runners I ran with and the courses we ran in 1979. You continue to be an inspiration to me on and off the course.

ABOUT THE AUTHOR

Bill lives in Western New York with his wife, Patty, and their two dachshunds, Brody and Herbie. He holds a Bachelor of Arts degree in biology and a Master of Science degree in leadership, both from Roberts Wesleyan University in Rochester, New York. After working thirty-two years in a manufacturing environment, he changed careers to gain a better understanding of servanthood, working almost twenty years in a maintenance and housekeeping capacity at the church he attends. Bill and Patty retired in 2024. He currently leads a small group gathering of Christians and periodically teaches a Bible study class.

Bill has been a Christian for most of his life, having been raised in the Free Methodist Church. As a junior in high school, he rededicated his life to Jesus Christ and affirmed his faith through baptism many years later as an adult. Retirement offers him more time to devote to his college sweetheart, Patty, genealogy research, and writing at his cottage by the lake.

Bill's writing coach, Yvonne Kanu, describes him as an "intentional storyteller who brings depth to seemingly everyday topics."

His books include the following:

Junior's Hope: A Memoir of a Father's Son (2006), written as a tribute to his deceased father. While journaling his father's last few months on Earth, Bill discovered his love for writing.

When the Dogs Bark: What My Dogs Taught Me about Relationships (2023), which spans twenty-six years of the author's life with dogs he has owned. He encourages readers to look at their relationship with dogs through a different lens and offers parallels to a relationship with God.

He maintains a blog, at www.billroushey.com.